BEYOND COLBY:

A Journey Into the Unknown

by

Charles "Chucky" Blanchard

Also by Charles "Chucky" Blanchard:
Colby Stories: Tales of a Paperboy (2008)

Acknowledgements

I am forever grateful and indebted to the following people who have helped and supported me along the way. And to the countless other people too numerous to mention who have encouraged me to write a book.

Patricia Palmer, for unlocking the other side and getting the ball rolling.

Dick Foster, for being my life long friend and resource for many stories.

Joan Fontanilla, for reading my stories and giving me excellent feedback.

Leslie Foster, for giving me encouragement and being a gentle guiding hand.

Jim Blanchard, for recalling all the times gone by and helping me remember how it was.

Jean Packard, for listening and encouraging her little brother.

Regine Kennedy, for being my editor and unconditional friend who turned fragmented stories into readable tales.

Sarah Davis, for drawing the book cover portrait and staying with me through the process.

Joanie, my loving wife who has helped me be all that I can be.

Aurelia Blanchard, my mother, who, upon viewing the drawer of my high school shop project and seeing the bottom of the drawer missing, said, "We will have to call you 'Board Short Blanchard'."

Every time I would get discouraged about finishing this book, I would look in the sky and say "Board Short Blanchard" lives no more.

Lisa Kelly, you have listened to my stories ever since we curled together in the 1990s. Thanks for all the encouragement and support.

Colby Readers, To all of you who have read my stories end encouraged me to write another book.

Forward

Chucky Blanchard's stories capture the essence of relationships while connecting us to the underlying wisdom and emotion. His first book, "Colby Stories: Tales of a Paperboy," was published in 2008.

When Charlie *(that's what I call him, I'm his wife.)* tells his stories, he captivates his audience—people laugh. His keen memory and total recall weave a tale till everyone is entertained. Reading Colby Stories, I often times wondered, "Did he make that up? Was that really their name?" After going to Colby for the funeral of his mother, and meeting all the town folk, it was confirmed.... he did **not** make up the names or stories.

His stories are simple, full, pieces of life that weave a tale—they are the stories that shape our lives.

I kept pushing Charlie to write a story about all that happened as a result of his first book being published. He finally got tired of listening to me and in a somewhat sarcastic way said, "I have an idea, why don't you write it?"

So here goes…this *of course is my perspective witnessing the events unfold.*

What a delight to have his first ever book-signing event

at our home. The table was filled with Colby cheese & Aurelia's (his mom's) strawberry shortcake recipe. What a surprise to discover, after tracing back into old family recipes from the1950s, it was still on the box of Bisquick in 2008.

So many friends and family members came to the book signing. What a tribute to the depth of friendships he has developed. After that event, when an order would arrive for a single copy, Charlie would meticulously sign each book, and hand deliver it to the post office. *(Before he wrote this book, Parkinson's had taken away his signature.)*

2008 was the year of his 45th Colby class reunion in Owen, Wisconsin. With his book in print, and a case in the car, we drove towards Colby for this event. Charlie wanted to make a stop or two before the reunion to hand deliver a gift to Mrs. Herrick. She was his first stop on his paper route some 55 years ago and he was sure she would still be there. (Really? I had a bit of wonder about this reality.) We drove to her home and, sure enough, her name was on the mailbox. Charlie walked up the steps, rang the bell, and when the door opened he said, "Mrs. Herrick I'm Chucky Blanchard your old paper boy." This tiny women of 90 years exclaimed, "Chucky Blanchard, you come right in. That Harry Feier used to always pick on you."

Mrs. Herrick's home hadn't changed one bit since the 50s and everything was neat and orderly. She received the gift of his book with pride and honor, holding it in her lap for the whole 15-minute visit and recalling more memories that were still so current in her mind. We heard through the grapevine how everyone at church the next day knew about Chucky's book!

Pearl Vorland used to be stop #2 on the paper route and lived next to Mrs. Herrick. Now, 55 years later, our next stop was a brand new development clear across town (about 20 blocks away). Pearl Vorland couldn't hear Chuck knocking or the doorbell for quite sometime because inside her vaulted great room, the large-screen TV was blasting. Once she did get to the door, Charlie once again said, "Hi Pearl. Do you remember me? I'm Chucky Blanchard your old paperboy. I wrote a book and wanted you to have one." "You! Wrote a book?" We were invited in to discuss book-writing and current events and heard some tales of all the people that gathered for Pearl's 95th birthday party, just a few weeks earlier. After excusing herself to freshen up for a photo I suggested, Pearl reentered the room with fresh makeup and wearing gold earrings. A gem of a photo was taken.

I witnessed the heartfelt love, consideration, and admiration two women from Colby received from Chucky Blanchard, their old paperboy. The feelings were mutual.

The 45th class reunion was almost anti-climatic after our heartfelt detour. Charlie was a little shy about bringing his book up and quietly told a classmate who made a grand announcement on his behalf. He trucked out to the trunk to bring in a case of books and promptly sold 26 books! (And yes, Timmy Schmidt, a way-back-when best friend mentioned in the book bought nine books, one for each of his children.)

In the fall of 2008, the library in Colby invited Charlie to visit for a book signing. In preparation for this event the Marshfield Herald featured a hometown author returning to Colby to once again deliver the paper. Charlie walked through a part of the old route delivering announcements of his book signing. The young reporter followed along and kept commenting how, "This delivery of the paper was a lot of work!" 55 years later, the paperboy from Colby was a front-page feature on the paper he used to deliver.

The book signing had a continuous line of residents filing in to buy a book. With every person's arrival, the room would fill with a beaming smile or a loud laughing recall of a memory from the past.

I stood in the background so proud to witness a part of Charlie's past as he in the present recaptured moments in time for all. I have been blessed to have taken this book-writing journey with Charlie.

As he started to put some of his tales on paper, I watched the creativity of this author and witnessed the balance of right brain /left brain thinking gives his body new directives to aid with his movement.

With this new book of stories, "Beyond Colby", you are invited to enjoy tales as he leaves his hometown from the bus depot in Abbotsford, Wisconsin and heads to the Twin Cities of Minneapolis and St.Paul with $412.68 and his suitcase and embraces his journey into the unknown.

Joanie Breen Blanchard

P.S. Copies of "Colby Stories: Tales of a Paperboy" are still available and *personally autographed.*

BEYOND COLBY

By
Charles "Chucky" Blanchard

TABLE OF CONTENTS

YOU TOO CAN BE AN EMBERS MANAGER TRAINEE

It was the summer of 1965. I was a twenty-year-old man working in Minneapolis with a lot on my mind. Three things happened that summer that would change my life forever - I received my draft notice, I became engaged, and I became an Embers Restaurant Manager Trainee.

Yes, I was going steady with Andrea Thomas and met her for a lunch date at the University of Minnesota.

"Well honey, it's May and I received my draft notice, I'll probably be in the Army by fall."

"I'll miss you Charlie, but if I don't have a ring on my finger, I won't be here when you get back."

Wow, I guess that meant we were getting married. So, off I went to Goodman Jewelers where I signed up for the EZ Payment Plan for $450. I presented the ring to Andrea, who seemed happy, but, after showing it to her mother, informed me that the ring wasn't big enough. So, back I went to Goodman Jewelers, where I picked another for $650. The salesman said, "Same EZ payments, but a longer term."

Well, I decided to have a meeting with myself and figure out my options. First of all, if I was going to marry a woman with expensive tastes, I needed a job that paid better than what I made as a radiator mechanic. I spotted an ad in the Minneapolis paper, "Manager Trainee Wanted – Terrific Income Potential – Call Duane Monette, Embers Restaurants, for an interview."

THE INTERVIEW:

I met Duane Monette, Regional Manager for Embers, at 2:45, fifteen minutes early for my 3:00 p.m. interview.

"Hello Mr. Monette, I'm Charles Blanchard."

He replied, "Call me Duane. May I call you Charlie?"

"Yes Duane, you can, and here's my resume."

Duane looked over my resume and kept saying "Great. Great. Great." and I kept wondering, "What's so great? I'm a twenty-year-old kid with no business experience who wants to be a manager." But Duane looked up and said "Charlie, you're just the guy I need. You have a small town background and so do I. Every kid I've hired from a small town is a good worker. Now let me explain how we're going to make you a manager. First, you need to learn every job in the restaurant - cooking, payroll, inventory, and employee supervision. In order to accomplish this, you'll have a pretty tough work schedule. The schedule is 6:00 p.m. to 6:00 a.m., six days a week, with Tuesdays off. While in training, the pay is seventy-five dollars weekly with a quarterly bonus of three hundred dollars. Just a minute. Look out the window. There goes one of our successful managers in that white

Mustang convertible. That's Bob Peterson and he'll be the person who trains you in. Well Charlie, if it looks like something you want to do, when can you start? After all, look at me, I started out as the janitor and now, eight years later, I'm the Regional Manager."

"Duane, I want the job, but I need to give MacAndrews Company a two-week notice, so I could start June first."

"Great. Great, Charlie. We'll see you at 6:00 p.m., June 1st. Welcome aboard."

I left that interview with great anticipation for the future. The hardest part would be explaining the long hours to Andrea. But anything worth attaining took a lot of hard work and I knew, eventually, I would be a good manager.

THE JOB:

I arrived fifteen minutes early at Guest House Embers to meet Bob Peterson and start my management course. Bob Peterson was all smiles and said, "We'll get the paperwork out of the way for payroll and get you started. Because we work twelve-hour shifts, you'll work with two shifts of waitresses. Get to know the waitresses because they can help you a lot. Let's get you started cooking."

I assisted all night with the bar rush and late-night diners. We cooked pancakes, steak and eggs, and lots of Embergers. Finally, at 2:00 a.m., we took a half-hour break and then started the daily inventory. Bob was a great teacher and motivator, if he had to correct me on anything, he would praise me on something else. And so it went. When 6:00 a.m. came, it was time to go home. I was very tired and very pleased with myself as I drove back to Grandma Nelson's house in Excelsior.

One of the benefits of working at Guest House Embers was that it was located across the street from Charlie's Café Exceptionale. Charlie's Café was the place to meet the rich, the politicians, and the colorful people. During the afternoon, Jerry, the maître d', would stop in and entertain us with stories of the previous night telling us which celebrity got drunk and said what to whom. During the early evening, two girls, Tracy and Susie, would tease me to see if I'd blush. Bob Peterson told me they were hookers, but I had to ask one of the waitresses, "What's a 'hooker'?"

Jean King replied, "Hookers get paid big money to do what most women do for free."

The nights rolled along and Bob said our numbers looked good and we should bonus. And bonus we did. In fact, our gross profit of 67.5 percent was the best in the company. We counted every lettuce leaf and made sure nothing went out the door that wasn't paid for.

In July of 1965, I took my draft physical and received notice three weeks later that I would be inducted into the Army on September 15, 1965. Embers took the news well and I was told that I would be a rotating Assistant Manager. That was okay with me since Bob Peterson was getting a store of his own in Anoka and the big profit guys were breaking up. My first assignment was at a brand new store on 26th and Hennepin in Minneapolis. On my first night, while I was doing the nine o'clock till check, I accidentally locked the keys in the till. I struggled to make change out of a cigar box for about an hour before a well-dressed man walked up to me and said, "Hi son, I'm Henry Kristal, one of the owners, and I think I can help you out."

Mr. Kristal took a key out of his pocket and unlocked the till. "It could happen to anybody, don't worry about it."

Then he left. I never will forget his act of kindness.

My final month before being inducted into the Army, was spent at the Nicollet Embers. This happened to coincide with the 1965 World Series and I can proudly say, I made it through the World Series cooking marathon! Dick Nordby, the manager, was right there with me the whole time getting the orders out. We had people lined up out to the street waiting for breakfast, lunch, and dinner. We worked fourteen to sixteen hour shifts and, on my way home, I picked up supplies from the other stores so we wouldn't run out of food. I worked right up to the day before I left for the Army. I felt, if I could handle Embers, I was ready for the Army.

THE END

P.S. Embers may have received cheap labor from me, but I received a great lesson in organization.

THE ARMY, GOD, AND ME

EXCELSIOR, MINNESOTA
SUMMER, 1965

Yes, it was a pretty good deal I had renting a room from Grandma Nelson in Excelsior, Minnesota. Twenty bucks a week, plus a dollar for every supper served and my laundry. However, now that I was working for Embers as a manager trainee, I pretty much ate all my meals at the restaurant.

I used to work for Grandma Nelson's son-in-law, Stan Kinghorn, as a radiator mechanic. Stan was fearful of the influence that the city might have on me, so he moved me in with his mother-in-law.

The draft board letter came about mid-July requesting that I report for an induction physical at the Federal Building in Minneapolis, Minnesota. "Well Grandma, I suppose I have a couple of years before I actually go in."

"Charlie, you have, at most, sixty days, based on the experience of my brothers in World War Two."

Grandma Nelson's words stuck with me and I knew I had to formulate a plan. I had no intention of dodging the draft, but I had to find out how to make the best out of my Army experience.

THE ARMY'S PLAN VERSUS MY PLAN

The Catholic Youth Center in Minneapolis was having a reunion of its co-ed softball team and among the attendees was Brad Schilling. Brad had just returned from Army basic training and couldn't wait to talk to me. "Let me tell you Charlie, the Army has a plan for you hunter-jock types and it isn't good. If you put down on the test that you like hunting and fishing, sure as hell, they'll put you in the infantry. The only two jobs you want are as a cook or Chaplain's Assistant. If you're lucky enough to become a Chaplain's Assistant, you go for five weeks training in California, then it's either Germany or Viet Nam, depending on your luck. In either case you won't be sucking mud in the infantry."

In that quick little conversation, I formulated my plan for how I would not only survive, but thrive in the Army.

THE INDUCTION PHYSICAL

The physical was short and sweet and all I remember is an Army Sergeant saying, "Mr. Blanchard, you have the flattest feet I have ever seen, but that won't keep you out of this man's Army."

I was given orders to report to the Milwaukee Road Railway Station at 0830 hours on September 15, 1965. Grandma Nelson's words were in my head "you will be gone in sixty days."

THE PARTING

I had recently become engaged to Andrea Thomas and she was not taking the news of me going into the Army very well. Her first reaction was to cry and wring her hands as she blamed the government for all troubles known to man. I suggested we could spend our time in a more romantic way. Andrea replied to that by going into the bedroom and coming out with two rosaries. I'm thinking to myself, "this certainly will be a long wait."

Finally, the time for departure came and it was a very tearful farewell when Andrea drove me to the train station.

RECEPTION STATION

We arrived at the Kansas City, Missouri train station around 7:00 p.m. and were ushered onto buses with a final destination of Fort Leonard Wood, Missouri. Over the next couple of days we were issued clothing and tested for our future military occupation. I couldn't wait for the testing to begin. The picture I would paint would not be of a gung ho war machine. The picture I would paint would be of a bookish cook who did not fish or hunt. I completed my testing and was waiting around the reception area when a Catholic priest came around asking for volunteers to be a Chaplain's Assistant. Well what could I say except, "Here I am Father. Here I am."

BASIC TRAINING

"Ok you ugly so-and-soes. Let's get into formation and double time. Huh!"

Those words were delivered by Staff Sergeant Porter, head drill sergeant. Sergeant Porter will be remembered as one of the greatest leaders I have ever met. He made what could have been a intimidating experience a very uplifting one. The only goal in Sergeant Porter's mind was to set a company record for the P.T. Test. You see, the Army has a test that consists of a mile run, grenade toss, belly crawl and obstacle course. The maximum score was 500 and Sergeant Porter had set the post record of 448. However, Sergeant Porter said, "We can't be satisfied with that. We must set a new record and show them who we are."

Our company name was D42 and when we marched we'd sing, "We are Delta, mighty, mighty Delta. Rough, tough Delta. Eat 'em up. Delta."

Yes, we were D42 and we were going to set a new P.T. Record. One day we were practicing the mile run and Sergeant Porter called out, "First three in get a three-day pass."

Up to that point in my life, I didn't know I was a runner, but when Sergeant Porter yelled, "GO!" I sprinted to the front of the pack and stayed there. When the race was over, Sergeant greeted me with, "Blanchard, you may not be the best marcher, but you are by far the best damn runner I've ever seen."

I found out a lot about my self that day and appreciated the kind words of Sergeant Porter.

Basic training was coming to an end and everybody was getting ready for the P.T. Test. The day came and went and D42 ended up with an average score of 491 and no 'BOLOS' (that means everyone in the company passed the test and we set a new post record). In the graduation speech Sergeant Porter said, "You men have made this the proudest day of my life. It has been my pleasure to lead you."

The next day I got my orders to report to Fort Ord, California for Chaplain's Assistant training.

CALIFORNIA HERE I COME

I had never been in an airplane before and there I was about to fly from Minneapolis to San Francisco. Accompanying me was a fellow that I met at the reception station, a very strong farm boy named Jim Bogner. Jim was from Crofton, Nebraska and had never been on a plane either. It was a fine ride with two stewardesses, Linda and Sally, entertaining us the entire way. Their attention was, however, more of a concerned nature than a flirtatious one. Sally confided in me that she was glad she was born a girl or she might be wearing an Army uniform too. We arrived safely in San Francisco and said good-bye to Linda and Sally.

CHAPLAIN'S ASSISTANT TRAINING, FORT, ORD, CALIFORNIA

Chaplain's Assistant training consisted of two weeks in Army Basic Administration and four weeks working as a Chaplain's Assistant. The Administration course was taught by women of the Women's Army Corps. The WACS were strict and mean, but I breezed through with a smile on my face and finished in the top five.

FATHER TONY SPIRELLA

I reported to the Fort Ord Catholic Chapel to meet my assigned priest, Father Tony Spirella.

"Just call me Father Tony young man. You can bet I'm not calling you

Private Blanchard, so what's your first name?"

"Charlie is my name and I'm your new Chaplain's Assistant."

"Well Charlie, for the immediate future you are the luckiest recruit on the planet. Let me explain the work schedule. Monday, Wednesday and Friday you cover the phones and I cover Tuesday and Thursday. On Sunday we both have to be here because that's 'Show Time'."

"But Father Tony, what will I do with all my free time."

"Well Charlie, you're a young man in the prime of his life living in southern California. I bet, if you put your mind to it, you can figure it out."

As I was leaving Father Tony said, "I noticed you eyeing my Mercedes and probably wondering about the vow of poverty. Well Charlie, my family has money and the car was a gift."

"I wasn't wondering Father, but it sure is a nice car."

Working with Father Tony was probably the best job I ever had. I spent most of the day typing letters to the families of soldiers who were experiencing problems adjusting to military life. Father Tony would interview the soldier and then write letters of counsel to the wives and parents. On my days off I made day trips to San Francisco, Carmel and Monterey taking in all the sites and enjoying the scenery. The only problem was that I kept running out of money. Alas, my age-old problem - my billfold always far behind my ideas.

THANKSGIVING IN SQUAW VALLEY

Jim Bogner stopped by the barracks and said, "My aunt Bonnie has invited me to visit for Thanksgiving weekend. The best part of it is that she said to invite a friend along. So, friend, do you want to go?"

"You bet Jim. I'm so broke I was just going to hang around the barracks anyway."

Aunt Bonnie picked us up in a brand new Cadillac wearing a Silver Fox fur coat and my eyes glazed over. I had never seen a more beautiful woman in my life and my blushing probably gave me away. Aunt Bonnie said, "Well boys, we're driving to Modesto then on to Squaw Valley for a weekend of skiing."

I said, "Sounds great!"

I couldn't help but wonder what Mr. Brady did for a living.

When we arrived in Modesto, I met the rest of the family, son Tom, age 19, and daughter Jenny, age 18, who winked at me when she shook my hand. Last, but not least, I met the father, Jack Brady. We stayed overnight at their beautiful home and then it was off to Squaw Valley. Jack and Bonnie Brady were great hosts and during the entire trip to Squaw Valley, Jenny kept smiling at me. I remember thinking, "Maybe she's just friendly."

When we arrived, we were put up in an enormous 'A'-frame cabin that slept twelve. The weekend was just great with lots of skiing under Jack Brady's suberb instruction. Jack was a former ski instructor who now made his living as a real estate developer. During the entire weekend Jenny was never more than a few feet away from me with a constant smile on her face.

On Saturday night I took a walk after supper and Jenny came running up behind me. This time the smile was gone from her face, replaced with a look of determination.

"Look Charlie, I talked to my dad and he says that you are a young man that'll be going places, so I think we should be going together."

"Wow!" I said, "That's all well and good, but I'm

engaged."

"Look around you. Where would you rather be than in a beautiful place like this with me?"

"I'm sorry, but all can say is 'I'm engaged' and I always keep my word."

Jenny said, "That's just my luck. Mom invites two guys up for the weekend and one is engaged and the other is my cousin."

Jenny went back to the cabin and never spoke to me again. The trip back to Modesto was not as joyful because everyone was smiling except Jenny. I said my good byes and Jenny just waved and ran back into the house. When I got back to the post I mailed a thank-you card, but I never heard from the Brady family again.

ANDREA & THE MUSTANG CONVERTIBLE

I received a letter from Andrea Thomas notifying me that she was flying out to see me the following weekend. No need to meet her at the airport, she said, she would rent a car. I talked it over with Father Tony and he arranged for a room in dependent housing. I was sitting by the barracks when Andrea pulled up in a white Mustang convertible.

"Going my way, soldier?"

The weekend was light and fun as we cruised up to San Francisco, stopping at Carmel. Overall, it was a fun weekend, but in the back of both our minds was the thought of where my next duty station would be. I would learn that destination in the next two weeks.

VIET NAM OR GERMANY?

Every soldier standing on the tarmac had one question on his mind. "Am I going to Viet Nam or Germany?"

The scuttlebutt from headquarters was that it would be a fifty-fifty split. The captain came down the line, stopping at every soldier to give him his orders. When he stopped in front of me, I was shaking in my boots. When he said, "Son, you're going to Germany," I almost kissed him. I immediately called Andrea and my folks with the news.

AUGSBURG, GERMANY DECEMBER 20, 1965

After a ten-day ship ride in the stormy North Atlantic, I arrived at my duty station – 2nd Battalion, 7th Artillery, Augsburg, Germany. My interview was with Lt. Col. Archibald P. Learch who, after he reviewed my file, said, "Please tell me what in hell I'm going to do with a Chaplain's Assistant?"

"Well sir, you should see me type. I can really type."

"Well, we have a clerk typist opening in Operations and I think you will do well there."

And well I did, rising to the rank of Sergeant and being nominated for the Army Commendation Medal.

THE END

The Army, God, and Me

GUARDING THE BEER BARRELS OF GERMANY

S-3 OPERATIONS DEPARTMENT, 7th ARTILLEY,
24th INFANTRY DIVISION
AUGSBURG, GERMANY
JUNE 1967

Well, I was indeed a short-timer in this man's Army. In sixty days I would board a plane for the good old USA. I'd been in Germany since November 1965 and working in S-3 Operations as Assistant Operations Sergeant since Bill Gaza went back to the States. Yes, the Army had been very good to me. I had risen from the lowly rank of Private up to Sergeant in only thirteen months. I have to admit it was all about being in the right place at the right time. When I arrived in Germany my Military Occupational Specialty, or MOS, was as a Chaplain's Assistant. The Battalion Commander, Lt. Colonel Archibald Learch, wasn't quite sure just what to do with me. I'd explained to him that I could type, "Boy, you should see me type." So the Colonel sent me to S-3 Operations on a trial basis. Let's go back and visit that time forty some years ago.

HOHENFELS FIELD PROBLEM:
HOHENFELS, GERMANY
NOVEMBER 1965

After an overnight stay at Headquarters in Augsburg, Germany, I was put on an Army truck heading up to Hohenfels training area in Central Germany. Hohenfels was where the Army practiced tactical maneuvers. As we arrived, I could see soldiers covered in mud and was glad I'd be working in an office. I walked into the operations office and was introduced to Sergeant Bill Gaza and Staff Sergeant Al Bungard. Sgt. Bungard, at six-foot five and two hundred forty pounds, was the boss and definitely too big to argue with. Bungard said, "Gaza will get you started typing the training schedule. I heard you can really type."

"Yes Sir. Get me started and I'll help you out any way I can."

In those ancient times, we would type on a stencil then run the papers off on a mimeograph. I completed the assignment, proofread it, and gave it to Sgt Gaza. Sgt Gaza said, "That was very quick, let's just see how many mistakes we have."

Sgt. Gaza looked up and said, "Looks good to me, chief."

Sgt. Bungard checked it over and said, "Charlie, you're quick, but, better yet, you're quick and accurate. Welcome to the Operations Department of the 7th Artillery. I think you're going to like it here. Now Sgt. Gaza, show Charlie where the coffee is since he'll be in charge of that too."

LIFE IN THE BARRACKS, SHERIDAN KASERNE: AUGSBURG, GERMANY

Now, growing up I wouldn't say I was the most spoiled kid, but I did have my own bedroom with lots of space. Since leaving home I'd always rented rooms in nice places and, when I lived with Grandma Nelson, I had a huge bedroom and a garage for my car. During the training phase of the Army, I could accept that we would live in crowded barracks, but I thought permanent duty quarters would be a lot better. I couldn't have been more wrong. There were nine guys crowded into a room only twelve by eighteen feet at most. All things being equal, it would've worked if alcohol weren't thrown into the mix. However, just about every other night, the two drunks, Pat Fergal and Paul Sears, would come into the room, after midnight, hollering and raising all kinds of hell. Finally, Sgt. Gaza mentioned the problem to Sgt. Bungard, who threatened to thump the hell out of Fergal and Sears. Needless to say, the harassment stopped.

A battalion has five hundred men. Each building on the post housed over a hundred men, so you can imagine the chaos when all five hundred men tried getting ready for five a.m. formation. But formation happened five days a week, attended by everyone except for a few soldiers who were AWOL (Absent With Out Leave). Then it was off to chow. Now, chow in the Army was very much dependent on where you were stationed. If you were in a large operation, such as ours, the food was terrible. The Army bought good food, but, by the time the Dehorn Cooks got done with it, it was inedible. I'd experienced the difference. One time, I pulled KP duty (Kitchen Police) in a small engineering unit in the States and the food was incredibly good. But then they were a small group of professionals and the Army wanted to take care of them. I had never pulled KP duty in Germany because Major Staruck called First Sergeant Shirley and told him I was needed in the Operations Department. I said to myself, "This must be what it's like to be a poor person - living close together and eating badly prepared food." I'd never thought of myself as rich before, but I'd grown up living in a nice house and eating like a king in comparison. I told myself, "This Army life isn't forever," and just made the best of every opportunity that came my way.

THE EXCHANGE RATE

From 1965 to 1967 the exchange rate was very favorable for soldiers because it was four Deutsch Marks to the U.S. Dollar. For example, you could buy a beer out of a vending machine for 50 pfennig's (twelve and one-half cents) or catch a ride downtown on the Strausobahn (street car) for one mark (twenty-five cents). Even a meal in a medium scale restaurant, a couple of beers included, would never run more than three bucks.

TRANSPORTATION

If you were enlisted personnel, meaning not an officer, you were not allowed to have a vehicle on post. That left the enlisted man to use public transportation such as the Strausobahn, taxis, or trains. Now the Strausobahn was really efficient and a bargain at twenty-five cents a ride. You could catch the old Strauss at Sheridan Kaserne and be downtown in twenty minutes. Taxis were quite a bit more expensive, at least five times more than the Strauss, so very few soldiers took them unless they were late for bed check and didn't want to get written up.

CURFEW AND BED CHECK

All enlisted personnel who lived on post were subject to a midnight bed check with no exceptions. Occasionally, deals were struck between soldiers, but that meant you had to get past the front gate. The front gate was closely guarded and, if a soldier came in late, the CQ (Charge of Quarters) at his unit was notified and the soldier was written up. Soldiers tried all kinds of ingenious ways to get back onto the post and avoid the gate guard. One soldier I knew found a little used door at the back of the post that had a rusty old lock on it. He sawed off the lock and replaced it with his own, thus gaining exclusive access. One late night he used the door and, once inside, he heard the guard shout, "Halt! Who goes there?" Well, this soldier knew no one was issued any ammunition, so he answered, "Only the shadow knows" and took off running to his barracks. The guard didn't pursue him, so one very quick-on-his-feet soldier made bed check with two minutes to spare.

ALBERT HOLGUIN SELF-APPOINTED BODY GUARD

The first soldier I met upon arriving in Germany was Albert Holguin. Even though we were from completely different backgrounds, we immediately became friends. Albert was a five-foot eleven, two hundred thirty pound brute. Everything was okay as long as Albert wasn't drinking. We went on passes all around Augsburg and met all kinds of people because Albert could speak German, Spanish, and Italian. Once we got away from the post, Albert conversed with many amazingly nice people and we had an entirely different perception on the country. Yes, Albert and I spent many a Saturday or Sunday traveling about the countryside, visiting with folks in the Gausthaus. We had great times. I never feared not speaking the language or running into bullies who would start fights, because we were American soldiers. Besides, Albert could translate three languages and the sheer size of him would put fear in the heart of any bully.

THE JOB

I started as the Operations Clerk and ended up being Assistant Operations Sergeant. The job had endless tasks that required me to work fifty hours a week, but even then, we never seemed to catch up. Operations handled, literally, every single aspect of running the battalion. We scheduled training and maintenance, requisitioned ammo supplies, secured training areas for five hundred men, coordinated transportation of five hundred men to and from the Hohenfels Training Area (a distance of three hundred miles) and on and on. My job was a hands-on, people sort of job that required excellent communication skills because I dealt with everyone from buck privates to full-bird colonels. I couldn't have had better teachers than Sergeant Bungard and Sergeant Gaza. Those guys took care of me like I was their little brother. When I think back to how we coordinated all this activity without computers or printers, it still amazes me. The fact that we could transport five hundred men, plus all their equipment, three hundred miles without losing a man or piece of equipment, is astounding.

THE SERGEANT SCHMIDT RELATIONSHIP

Early in my career I was assigned to coordinate with Sergeant Schmidt of the Augsburg Police. My initial question to the Sergeant was, "Coordinate what?"

"Well Charlie, it works like this. Every officer and non-commissioned officer is rated on the overall conduct of the men under their command. That means, if one of their men is arrested by the Military Police, the officer receives a 'Gig' on his personnel review. The Army believes that real leaders will inspire their men to serve and not get in trouble. Now, in Headquarters Battery, we have secured a secret weapon in the person of Sergeant Schmidt of the Augsburg Police. I've been in the Army twenty-one years and I can pretty well predict who will get into trouble. I tell those guys, if they are arrested, to ask for Sergeant Schmidt. Sergeant Schmidt will then call you and you'll go and pick the guys up from jail. That way, no Military Police, no Court Martial for the soldier, and no 'Gig' on the Commanding Officer's personnel file. As for Sergeant Schmidt, my wife is his cousin and we pay him off in coffee and brandy. Schmidt is a crafty old dude, so he might hit you up for an additional payment. Just stand strong and tell him Sergeant Bungard will take care of him on the weekend."

About two weeks later I was on CQ when the phone rang. I answered, "Headquarters, Second Battalion, 7th Artillery. Sergeant Blanchard speaking, Sir."

It was Sergeant Schmidt. "Hello Sergeant Blanchard, this is Sergeant Schmidt, Augsburg, Police and I have a couple of your boys down here in the holding cell."

"Can you tell me their names Sergeant?"

"Yes. We picked up these two dumkuffs before. It's Paul

Sears and Pat Fergal."

"Okay Sergeant. I'll pick them up in about an hour."

I got off shift and drove down to the police station and picked up two, very grateful, but still drunk, soldiers. Sergeant Schmidt said, "I'm getting low on coffee and brandy."

I said, "Sergeant Bungard will be over this weekend."

GET YOUR GED

One day I was talking to Sergeant Bungard about goals and accomplishments and said, "We must do more than rescue drunks from the Germans."

"Well Charlie, what do you have in mind?"

"Well Sarge, let's check the personnel file of all the soldiers in Headquarters Battery and see who hasn't graduated from high school. Then we can gather these guys in the conference room and I will give them a little presentation on the value of a high school diploma."

"Okay Charlie, sounds like a good plan to me, but I sure hope these knuckleheads don't disappoint you."

"I'll take my chances Sarge and see if I can't get these guys going in the right direction."

The next morning, Sergeant Bungard reviewed the files and thirty-three men of the one hundred five in our unit had not graduated from high school. I passed out fliers to the men in question and twenty showed up at the seminar. My guest speaker was the post's education officer, Captain Bradley.

He explained the benefits of graduating and how they could take all the necessary courses by correspondence. Then he explained that, if anyone needed tutoring, they could go to the education center where Sergeant Blanchard would help them out.

Well, after a year, of the twenty men that signed up, twelve graduated and received their GED. Sergeant Bungard said, "I thought you would be lucky if you got two."

Captain Bradley was very pleased and recommended me for the Army Commendation Medal. I felt it was tough job and was very pleased that I thought of it and followed through with Captain Bradley.

LUIGI THE BARBER

In the Army a haircut is very important. Every battalion has its own barber and we had one of the best. His name was Luigi. Luigi had worked as General Mark Clark's barber during World War II and no soldier could ever pull the wool over his eyes. One time I was sitting, getting a haircut, and asked Luigi, "What would you do if the Russians ever invaded and took over Germany?"

Luigi said, "No problem. Instead of drinking the whiskey, I would just drink the vodka."

Yes, rolling with the punches was a definite strong suit of Luigi's.

ALERTS

Everybody in the Army hates alerts because they catch you off guard and, basically, throw everyone into a panic. Generally, an alert is called between midnight and four in the morning and the whole battalion has to pack up everything and leave the Kaserne. When I say everything, I mean everything. Every man, every rifle and every piece of equipment had to go. In the case of Operations, we had three safes containing intelligence data that had to be lugged down two flights of stairs and stored safely in an Army Personnel Carrier. Once assembled, it was off to a secret destination to be reassembled in the mountains. The only perk about alerts was that we were doing this in southern Bavaria, one of the most beautiful places on earth. Once, I overheard two soldiers moaning and complaining as they sat in the pine forest eating their breakfast and waiting for the end of the alert. I thought to myself, "we could be doing this in Viet Nam and it would be a whole different story".

One day, I bumped into Tommy Anderson from Austin, Minnesota who was in boot camp with me at Fort Leonard Wood, Missouri. Tommy said, "I know in advance what time and day they're calling the alerts."

"How do you know that Tommy?"

"I have a German girlfriend who works for the Highway Department. Every time they call an alert, the Army calls in for road clearance. Next month I'll call you, Charlie, with a code for the day of the alert. It'll be, 'the Schnitzel is hot at 2:30', which means the alert will be at 2:30 a.m. the following morning."

"Say no more about it Tommy. I'll wait for the call."

And call Tommy did. I shared this intell only with my boss, Sergeant Bungard. Even knowing the date and time, however, didn't make the alert any easier. Ask any soldier who served in Germany how they like the alerts and watch their eyes cloud with a dreaded memory.

ORPHANAGE CARNIVAL

I sat down with my Commanding Officer, Captain Ballah, one day and observed that the average German citizen was getting a bad view of the average American soldier.

"You see, Sir, these kids come over here as teenagers, get all liquored up on their first pass and raise hell with the Germans. I have a counter plan for that image and would like your help to make it happen. You see, Sir, I would like the men of this battalion to put on a carnival for a local orphanage."

"Well Charlie, I have no objection to that. Get with Sergeant Bungard, since he speaks fluent German, contact the local orphanage and I'll help you any way that I can."

I ran the plan by Sergeant Bungard and told him that I had the blessing of Captain Ballah. The Sergeant arranged for a meeting with the nuns at a Catholic orphanage in Freistag,

Germany, about fifteen miles away. I understood very little of what was said, but the nuns and Sergeant Bungard were doing a lot of smiling, so I figured everything was good. Sergeant Bungard said, "All set. The date is Saturday, October 30 with thirty orphans, fifteen boys and fifteen girls. Now we have to line up thirty couples, because I promised a couple escort for every child."

We went back to Operations Headquarters, got on the phone and lined up the couples. We even hired a German clown and a man who had a spider monkey. Sergeant Bungard said, "My wife's cousin works for the Freistag paper, it wouldn't hurt to give him a call."

Captain Ballah came in and said, "You guys are a couple of Barnum & Bailey's. I was at the PX and everybody is talking about it. Keep up the good work."

The carnival went off without a hitch, due in great part to the generosity of the soldiers and their wives who were very attentive to the children. Both the clown and the monkey handler were big hits and all the children seemed to have a good time. A newspaper reporter and a photographer showed up and took some pictures, so, all in all, things turned out pretty good.

Two days later, Sergeant Bungard came in with the paper and said, "Look Charlie, you got your picture in the paper with one of the children."

I picked up the paper, all set to read it, but, of course, it was in German. Sergeant Bungard said, "Give it back.

I'll read a synopsis. 'The Nuns at Freistag Orphanage are very thankful for the generosity and kindness shown by the soldiers of 2nd Battalion, 7th Artillery.' It goes on to talk about the carnival and is very hopeful that it will be an annual event. You should feel good about this one Charlie. You really did a lot of good."

"Well Sarge, I never could've done it without you and Captain Ballah. We did well. We all did well."

HOMEWARD BOUND

On August 31, 1967, I arrived at the Minneapolis Airport wearing my full dress uniform and passed a young soldier who looked like he'd just got out of boot camp. The soldier yelled at me, "LIFER!" ('Lifer' is a derogatory term for a career soldier). I walked over and said. "No young man, I'm all done. Now it's your turn."

THE END

Written: October 2, 2006

OH PLEASE MR. SWANSON, LISTEN TO MY CANARY SING

CUSTOMER ACCOUNTING OFFICE, MINNEGASCO
MINNEAPOLIS, MINNESOTA
SEPTEMBER 15, 1967

Well here I am, fresh out of a two-year stint in the Army and back working in an office. While I was still in the Army, I'd sent a resume to Howard Johnson's Restaurants applying for a Manager Trainee Position. Howard Johnson's sent me a letter and said to apply at the local Howard Johnson's in St. Paul as soon as I was discharged from the Army. So, I arrived home on Thursday, interviewed on Friday and started with Howard Johnson's the following Monday. It didn't take me but a day to figure that this job wasn't a manager trainee job, but cheap labor under the disguise of management trainee. You didn't really cook anything from scratch - every ingre-dient for the meal was prepared in Chicago and then shipped up by truck to all the Howard Johnson's in a five state area. So the cooks really didn't cook anything, they just heated up what the trucks brought in. So, by the time Tuesday came around, I changed my goals and decided I would rather work in an office. I quit my job at Howard Johnson's and spotted an ad in the newspaper for a job in customer accounting with Minnegasco.

THE JOB AND THE JOURNEY

Basically, the job in customer accounting was taking incoming calls from customers. Most were complaints about high bills. About fifty people worked the phone, of those, forty-nine were men and one was a pioneering woman by the name of Sharon Landmark. Some of the guys resented Sharon because she was a little pushy, but, overall, she was readily accepted as one of the crew.

The calls would come in fast and furious during May, the moving season, and it was important that the new information was entered correctly. Now, keep in mind, that this was 1967 and just the dawning of the computer. Imagine, if you will, a big, open room with over a hundred people in it, all talking on the phone. Also, this was a time when just about everyone smoked and the company allowed you to smoke at your desk. Yes, those were the sixties, the good old days, a hundred people yacking away with a blue haze of smoke rising about five feet above the floor.

Can't imagine how we ever lived through it, but we did and a great change eventually came.

THE MAIL RUN

Prior to getting trained on the phones, Minnegasco required new employees to complete a two-week tour of the mail run. This tour amounted to delivering the mail to all of the offices on the three floors that the company occupied and preparing all of the utility bills for mailing. My trainer was Tom Schinn and he was as nervous as a hooker sitting in the middle of a Methodist Church.

"Now Charlie, they'll be grading you on the amount of time it takes you and if you deliver the mail to the wrong person."

Everything went well for the first week and a half and on Friday of the second week, I was going to make my graduation run. The night before, I ran it all through my mind and it was my intention to make it a record run. Unbeknown to me at the time, the only person keeping track of any of it was old nervous Tom Schinn.

Friday came and I took the elevator down to the first floor to pick up the mail for the day. I had it all planned out. The first stop was Jack Marx, Vice President of Advertising, and then quickly next door to Paul Kramer in the president's office. Yes, quickly and efficiently, that's how I needed to move to make the best run ever. Then it was off to the Customer Accounting Department where I would make my mark. The elevator pulled up and I saw Jack Marx's beautiful secretary sitting there with a bee-hive hair-do that was stacked to the sky. No time for chit-chat, I needed to drop off the mail. Unfortunately, my mind was ahead of my body and instead of backing up and walking into Jack Marx's office, I pivoted and walked through a plate glass wall. Instinctively, I went into a wrestler's crouch then all I heard was glass breaking and Jack Marx's secretary screaming for help. I sure didn't feel like a dying man and, other than the screaming secretary, the breaking glass, and being scared, I felt pretty good. I brushed myself off and noticed that all I had was a small cut on my arm. The people around me weren't quite as sure because Jack Marx's secretary went pale and looked like she'd witnessed a murder. Even old Jack Marx was taken aback and came out to say, "I hope you're all right, son."

The security guard rushed me off to Thelma Johnson, the company nurse, and Thelma examined me in her office.

"Well Charles," Thelma said, "did you have your breakfast today?"

"Yes, Ms. Thompson, I did, but I don't know what happened. One second I was outside of Jack Marx's office, and the next I was through the glass wall."

"Do you think you want to go home for the rest of the day, Charles?"

"No Ms. Thompson, I want to get back and finish my mail route because I start on the phones in Customer Accounting on Monday."

"Well Charles, you seem fine, but I would keep an eye out and if you feel dizzy or queasy, come back and see me."

"Yes, I will." I said, "I'll be careful and keep an eye out."

When I arrived back at Customer Accounting, everybody looked like they expected to see a dead man, but this look of shock and concern soon turned into laughter and ridicule. I kept my cool about me, but was shocked when the Minneapolis Police Department stopped by to see, as they described me, the "Human Torpedo". After a couple weeks of teasing it all died down and I settled into my new job in Customer Accounting and never went near Jack Marx's office again.

THE EVER PRESENT UNION

The office workers of Minnegasco were represented by the International Office Employees Union. This was the first and last union to which I ever belonged. You might wonder why I take such a hard line, but I think a union is like having a drunken brother-in-law over for dinner - they take your earnings and never offer anything in return. Unfortunately, it wasn't a matter of choice if you worked at Minnegasco, you had to join the union. I paid my dues and kept my opinions to myself. Then came election day for the union officers. The union steward came by with a list of strongly suggested candidates for me to vote for. That did it for me. From that point on, I didn't think of the union and, when it came time to vote, I picked my candidates by choosing names I liked. Whether or not my union steward caught on, he never let me know. The only time I thought of the union was when I saw the dues being taken out of my paycheck for no good purpose. Thank God that was the only union job I ever had.

One year later, when I was interviewing for a job with

GMAC, the first thing I asked was if employees had to belong to a union. When they said, "No", I said, "I'm your man."

I would be less than honest if I didn't admit that the raises won by the United Auto Workers, and passed on to the administrative employees at GMAC, were never turned down by me. Still, in my opinion, unions remain more like politicians than like the workers they represent.

HANNAH NELSON AND HER CANARY

Jerry Swanson was a very likable chap and, during the years he worked at Minnegasco, was very entertaining to the customers. In fact, if a customer had a Scandinavian name, Jerry would go into his Swedish brogue and say, "Yah. Sure. You betcha. We can help you out with dat."

Where Jerry Swanson met his match was when he was talking to Hannah Nelson and her canary named Jerry. Hannah would call in under the premise that she had a high bill complaint and end by tying Jerry Swanson up on the phone for an hour. At the very end of the conversation, Hannah would say, "You just got to hear my canary sing."

Jerry would reply that the calls were backing up, but he would finally give in and listen to the melodious canary warble away. After he finally got off the phone, his supervisor would give him a hard look and Jerry would say, "We can't be rude to the customer."

These calls would come in nearly every day, but, some-times, the girls at the switchboard would tell Hannah that Jerry was sick. Hannah would not be deterred and would call back later in the day saying she had a special message for Mr. Swanson and would get right through. Once she got Jerry on the phone, she would offer to bring him chicken soup to cure what ailed him. "After all, I can't let my best Minnegasco representative get sick on me can I? By the way, my canary is in rare form. Would you mind listening to him sing?"

Then one day Jerry came in and said, "I'm tired of winter. I'm moving to Florida."

Two weeks later Jerry Swanson was gone and the rest of us were left with Hannah Nelson and her singing canary. Gary Pygman, the supervisor, said, "Oh boy. What are we going to do about Hannah?"

Then Gary looked up at me and said, "Charlie say 'Yah. Sure. You Betcha.'"

"Oh no. You're not going to stick me with Hannah."

"I'm sorry Charlie, but you do the best voices, so I'm afraid you're the best man for the job."

The next morning I answered the phone, "Minnegasco Customer Accounting, Jerry Swanson speaking."

The switchboard had alerted me ahead of time so this was 'Act One'.

"Oh Swanee, your voice sounds so much better. Are you done being sick now?"

41

"Yah. Sure. You betcha Hannah. I'm fit as a fiddle since my ma made me some chicken soup."

"Oh Swanee, I thought your mother died in the flood by Mankato."

"No. Ma showed up floating on a piano bench and she is fine as rain. And pretty fit, I might add, for a woman of eighty-seven."

"Wow Swanee. She's the same age as me. I could be your mother."

"You just never know Hannah. By the way, how is your canary doing?"

"He's doing just fine. Let me put him on and you can hear him sing."

And that's how it went until a year later when I left Min-negasco for another job. I don't know who took my place as 'Swanee', but I hope he treated Hannah and her canary well. I think the lesson to be learned here is that if you have any-body elderly in your family, and you haven't talked to them in awhile, give them a call. If it's inconvenient to call, buy a funny card and send it to them. Remember, humor and kind-ness go hand in hand in a well-balanced life.

JAMES STASNEY, THE LAZIEST MAN I EVER MET

Everyone in the Customer Accounting Department at Minnesgasco was partnered up with a more experienced person sitting next to them. If you just started, the person in the desk next to you probably had five years experience. This plan was to ensure that the customer inquires received a prompt and correct answer. It was my misfortune to be partnered up with James Stasney, the laziest man I've ever met. James Stasney was twenty-six going on ninety-four and he rarely took a phone call. If he would get a call, he would say to the caller, "Mr. Blanchard will be right with you."

The reason Mr. Blanchard couldn't answer was because Mr. Blanchard was busy taking all the other calls. I was silly enough to believe that, if I set a good example, Stasney would be shamed into working. Wrong! James Stasney was a lazy bum and he knew that, as long as he was in the union, he didn't have to work, he just had to show up. Finally, one day I just asked him. I said, "Mr. Stasney, is there one definite reason that you let me do all the work?"

"Yes Mr. Blanchard, there is. I have five years seniority with the union, so I don't have to."

"Don't you kind of feel like a burden on the company with your attitude?"

"Mr. Blanchard, I don't really care, and, by the way, here's another call coming in for you."

So I continued trying to set a good example for Stasney, but his work habits never improved. He just sat there taking up space.

One day, I was walking on Marquette Avenue in front of Minnegasco and saw old Stasney walking in front of me carrying a paper bag. A muskrat's tail was hanging out of the back of the bag, so, apparently, there was a muskrat inside the bag. I caught up to Stasney and said, "I got to ask. Where are you going with that muskrat?"

"Oh, Mr. Blanchard. I'm off to Berman Buckskin to sell it."

"If Berman doesn't buy it, are you bringing it back to the office?"

"But of course. What would you expect me to do?"

"I wouldn't expect you to bring a dead muskrat to the office, but we'll see you later."

About an hour later, Stasney showed up at the office, less the muskrat, with a big grin on his face. "Berman gave me $1.75 for the muskrat. What do you think of that?"

"Mr. Stasney, I don't think the life of a professional trapper is in your future and you need loftier goals."

Stasney said, "Oh well. By the way, another call is coming in."

A few months later James Stasney met a woman at a Bible Study group who was thirty-two years his senior and married her. On his last day of work, Stasney said, "My wife has a lot of money and she doesn't want me to work. Mr. Blanchard I told you I was never going to work again."

TIME TO GO

In October of 1968, I interviewed for a Field Representative position with GMAC and was hired to start October 15,

1968. I gave my notice to my supervisor, Gary Pygman, and he said, "We'll miss you, but, more importantly, who is going to be Jerry Swanson?"

"I don't know Gary, but I'd start the selection process now. Hannah is still going strong."

On my last day my co-workers presented me with a leather brief case tied with a white ribbon. The names of all the people I worked with were written on the ribbon. The other night, I pulled out a folder and there was the ribbon still intact after thirty-eight years.

THE END

Written: November 16, 2006

THE REPO MAN

It was July of 1968 and I was working as a Customer Service Rep with Minnegasco in Minneapolis, Minnesota. Minnegasco provided natural gas service to the residents of Hennepin County and it was my job to handle all the high bill complaints. All in all, it wasn't a bad job, but it was pretty boring. Unfortunately, in addition to being boring, all employees had to belong to the Inter-National Office Workers union. No one in my whole family had ever belonged to a union and I didn't like the idea of anyone speaking for me. I came to the conclusion that I needed to look for a better job with a better future.

Then, one day, one of my co-workers came in all dressed up in a nice suit. "What's with the fancy duds, Howie?" I inquired.

"Charlie, I just gave my two week notice. I got a job with Aetna Insurance. I'm going to train to be an adjustor and my starting pay is twenty-five percent more than I'm making here."

Howie explained that he got the job through Employment Advisors Agency. He gave me their phone number and said, "I think they might need another good man."

I called Brian Olson at Employment Advisors and set

up an interview for the next day at noon. Brian met me in the reception area with my resume in hand. He said, "I have looked everything over and I have two strong opportunities. The first job is for a Production Manager for an agricultural supplier and the second is as a Field Representative for GMAC."

I said, "Line me up an interview with both companies."

Brian called the next day and said, "Minnesota Ag Products is at 10:00 a.m. and GMAC at 2:00 p.m. next Thursday."

INTERVIEW: MINNESOTA AG PRODUCTS

Harley Henderson, Vice President of Minnesota Ag Products, met me for the interview. I was taken aback by his youthful appearance. Harley, at about twenty years old, had a moppy head of blonde hair and dressed like a teenager. Well, I had come this far, but felt funny being all dressed up in a blue suit with a fancy tie and shiny wing tip shoes. We sat down and Harley started to read out of a book called, 'Interviewing for Results'. Harley said, "According to this book, when we're finished, I will know more about you than you do."

I took it for a few questions, but then I interrupted and said, "This interview is over. You see, I've been around. I'm twenty-three years old and I had a 'Secret' clearance in the Army. If you think I'm going to let some kid interview me from a book, you're crazy."

I walked out and called Brian, who was none to thrilled, at the agency and prepared for GMAC.

INTERVIEW: GMAC

"Hello Charlie, I'm Dean Mundy," said the well-dressed man in the gray suit, "And I will be interviewing you for the Field Rep position."

Mr. Mundy led me into a plush office and the journey began. He explained that the job involved consumer collections, on the phone and in person, in addition to conducting wholesale audits. Then he added, "As a Field Rep, you will have the use of a General Motors company car."

Once a company car was mentioned, I was bound and determined to get the job. We discussed my present job and Mr. Mundy assured me that I would not have to join any union to work there. I told him, "I definitely want the job and await your decision."

Mr. Mundy replied that he had other candidates but would let me know in a couple of days. I had just got back to the office when he called and offered me the job. He said, "Give your notice today and you can start work on September 15. You will have a six-month training period in the office and then you will be out in the field driving a new company car."

By golly my plan was coming together. I was only twenty-three, had a brand new house, was married and, maybe, I would make Vice President by the time I was thirty-five.

TELEPHONE CREDIT MAN

In September 1968, I started my first day on the job as a Telephone Credit Man. I called delinquent accounts from 11:00 a.m. to 7:00 p.m. to get acquainted with the debtors. My supervisor, Bob Engler, was a crusty old character who taught me the dos and don'ts of working with credit customers, "Always be firm, but polite and don't get off the point of your call."

I faithfully did my job for six months and then, one day, Bob Engler said, "A Field Rep position just opened up and I recommended you for the job. Stop by and see me and I'll help you with your initial reports."

Bob had a tear in his eye and looked like a man sending his son off to war not a crusty old collection manager. The next day I picked up a brand new 1969 Blue Chevrolet Impala at Jay Kline Chevrolet and started working my new territory.

MY FIRST REPO

General Motors is almost as big as the government and, like the government, has a form for almost every situation. The form that strikes fear into the heart of any Field Rep is Form 582. A 582 is an interbranch collection assignment with simple instructions: 'Collect in Full, Extend Payments or Repossess the Collateral'. Do one of the three, but it must be done within twenty-four hours. So, whatever else is going on in your territory, the 582 takes top billing. My first 582 read as follows:

CUSTOMER: LEROY JARVIS
ADDRESS: 2622 EMERSON AV N. MINNEAPOLIS, MN
COLLATERAL: 1968 OLDS 98. CALIF PLATES
INSTRUCTIONS: CUSTOMER LIVING WITH PRO BOXER
PAT RYAN.
CUSTOMER PRO BOXER, 6'2, 211 LBS. MEAN NEGRO.
DO NOT CONTACT. REPO ON SIGHT.

Well, this repo was going to test my creativity and ingenuity and, since it was my first, I wanted the company to remember it. Bob Engler gave me the number for Dorothy in Detroit and I called her to get the key number to the Olds. Key number in hand, I went to Lindahl Olds and told the parts man to be real careful cutting this one.

I arrived at 2622 Emerson about 9:00 a.m. and immediately spotted the Olds parked on the street. I parked my car on a side street and snuck up to the passenger side of the car. Just as I tried the key in the door I heard the two boxers coming out of the house. I froze and tried to think what my next move would be. Then I heard Leroy say, "Damn! We forgot to call Jimmy."

Both boxers turned around and went back into the house. I jumped in the Olds and gunned it through a red light with the engine back firing all the way back to the repo lot. When I got to the lot, I called the Police, learning that Leroy had reported the car stolen, and called a cab to get a ride back to my company car. When I arrived at the office, both boxers were arguing with Bob Engler, but Bob said, "Payment in full. In cash. Or no car."

Leroy said to Bob Engler, "Just answer me one question. How in the world did your Rep find me in the first place?"

"Well sir, you are a finely trained boxer and our Reps are highly trained investigators. Exactly how he did it, I can't tell you, but spread the word, if you don't pay, GMAC will always find you."

What Bob didn't tell Leroy was that we had paid off someone at the phone company in Oakland, California to monitor the origin of all incoming long distance calls to Leroy's home in Oakland. Once Oakland GMAC branch saw consistent calls from Minneapolis they traced the number and I was there the very next morning.

THE END

P.S. More Repo stories coming soon!

The Repo Man

ME AND MIKE AGAINST THE WORLD
Tales of a Repo Man

In the fall of 1969, I was working as a Field Rep for GMAC out of their Minneapolis Branch. It was a tough year for us because Reps were quitting right and left. One morning I came into the office and the Collection Manager, Frank Brown, said, "Go ahead and introduce yourself to the new guy. His name is Mike McClellan."

Unbeknownst to me, our Branch Manager, Jim Everline, had had a liquid lunch and had already introduced himself to Mike three times. I walked over and Mike jumped up to introduce himself. I don't know if it was his crazy laugh or the twinkle in his eye, but I knew Mike would be fun to work with.

"Nice to meet you Mike. You'll be riding with me tomorrow. We'll be doing an audit and maybe some field collection calls. I'll see you in the morning at nine a.m."

"No problem, Charlie. I'll be here on time, ready to go."

Frank Brown, the Credit Supervisor, called us over to his desk. "Look Charlie, there's no overtime, any time, for trainees. So tomorrow, if you get close to eight hours, drive Mike back to his car."

AUDITS: LOVE THEM OR HATE THEM

General Motors Acceptance Corporation (GMAC) financed the wholesale inventory of General Motors' dealerships. My job, as a Field Rep, was to conduct physical inventories and records checks to make sure dealers weren't selling 'out of trust'. That is, when a dealer sold a car, he had twenty hours to pay off GMAC or they were 'out of trust'. It all boiled down to the dealer's financial stability. If they were a strong, well-run organization, they rarely ran 'out of trust'. But, if they were loose and financially weak, they had more moves than a belly dancer.

General Motors management didn't care if the dealers were cooperative or uncooperative, they wanted a complete audit done in twenty-four hours. The message was loud and clear, "Get the audit completed, no matter what." Some dealers thanked me for verifying that their inventory was correct and some dealers treated me like a bum. I kept my cool and a smile on my face knowing that my supervisor, Frank "Nails" Brown, would back me up. Frank was tough, but fair, and had little time for 'out of trust' dealers.

TRAINING THE TRAINEE

I picked up Mike McClellan at the office at nine a.m. and explained that we were doing an audit at Borgman Chevrolet. I explained, "The former Field Rep, George Pfeifer, really ruffled the owner's feathers. My last experience here was very testy. The best I can tell you is this - only deal with the bookkeeper. I'll deal with the salesman."

Mike and I each had a copy of the audit, so we split up and started the physical inventory. We were done in about two hours, ending up with a list of missing cars. Then it was time to sit down with the head bookkeeper, Ruth Ellen Shapiro, who, incidentally, insisted on being called 'Ruth Ellen'. I left Mike to go over the sales receipts with Ruth Ellen while I checked the street and the body shop for missing cars. After my search, I went to the New Car Manager's office to talk to Art Loecker. Mr. Loecker was in a foul mood and told me, "Just keep looking until you find them."

"Well, Mr. Loecker, I'll have to call my supervisor and ask him how to proceed."

"Now you just go ahead and do that, but, for now, get out of my hair."

I called Frank Brown and explained the situation. Frank went wild saying, "We own those demos and we need to inspect them. Tell Mr. Loecker to have all the demos lined up by eight-thirty tomorrow morning or he is 'out of trust'. If he can't do that, he should have a check ready to pay them off."

"Okay Frank, but if he shoots me, please say nice things at my funeral."

I decided imminent death could wait and went to check on Mike. He was having a grand time checking the books with Ruth Ellen and Ruth Ellen was completely mesmerized by our twinkly-eyed Irishman. I was very pleased that at least something was going right. I took Mike aside and told him about my conversation with Frank Brown. Mike said, "Goodness gracious! I'll warm up the get away car."

I gave Mike the keys to the company car and told him, "Meet me in ten minutes."

Art Loecker walked by and I told him that I needed to see him, alone, in his office. I explained the company's position, "The long and short of it is, I need to see all the demos tomorrow, at eight-thirty a.m., or pick up a check for $36,284.00."

Art stared at the floor for a minute, then looked up and said, "They'll be here."

"Thanks for your cooperation. I'll see you in the morning."

LUNCH AT THE AMBASSADOR

As soon as I got in the car, Mike said, "If you like pretty girls, let's go to the Ambassador for lunch. Patty Floyd, a friend of my sister, Rita, is a cocktail waitress there and she's pretty as a movie star."

"Okay. Let's go Mike. After dealing with these car salesmen, I could use a good lunch."

Mike hadn't been exaggerating. Patty Floyd was very pretty. Oh, and the Ambassador put out a great lunch too. Mike asked, "Can we put this lunch on our expense account?"

"No way. You have to have been traveling overnight before the big GM will cover. Let's finish up and go on a collection call."

Patty stopped by our table, "Good luck on today's adventure. Charlie, you take good care of Mike."

Then it was off to South Minneapolis to teach Mike about collections in the field.

THE COLLECTION CALL

GMAC issued its collection assignments on Form 571. The form included: Customer Name, Address, Make & Model of Vehicle and account status. I handed a 571 to Mike and said, "Read it over, then I'll answer any questions you have."

"Okay. Customer Tom Schmidt. Sixty days past due on a 1968 Chevrolet, one-ton truck. He lives at 3921 Bloomington Avenue in Minneapolis, Minnesota."

As we pulled up to the customer's house, I could see that our truck wasn't there. However, the porch window was open and I could hear the radio inside. I knocked on the door and a woman in her late twenties answered. "Mrs. Schmidt, I'm Charlie Blanchard from GMAC and this is Mike McClellan. We're here to see Tom about his account.

"Listen. I'm his girlfriend. The reason Tom's behind is that he's too busy working to get his checkbook straightened out."

Mike pipes in with, "You mean he's too busy to keep track of his own money?"

Then he laughed. I tried to smooth it over, but the unidentified girlfriend was much taken aback and offended by the remark. I said, "Here's my card. Please have Tom call me."

Once we were in the car I explained to Mike that smart aleck remarks wouldn't help the situation. "Think anything you want, but don't offend the customer."

Well it was nearing four-thirty and time to get Mike back to the office before he went into overtime. I'd go back to the Schmidt residence at seven p.m. to try and resolve the delinquency.

When I arrived later that night, I had a strange feeling that it wasn't going to be easy pickings. As I got closer, I could see Tom Schmidt sitting on his porch. He looked mean and drunk. As soon as his eyes met mine, he said, "You're the prick who insulted my girlfriend."

"No. That wasn't me. I apologize for my associate's remark."

At that moment, Tom lunged for me and pushed me through the hedge. As I was going through, I caught my suit pants and tore a hole in the knee. Tom was after me and ready to do some serious damage, but all I could think about was my new suit with a hole in the knee. Tom came at me again. I lowered into a wrestler's crouch and tackled him, sending him back through the hedge. Tom looked up and said, "That's enough Mr. GMAC man."

"No," I said, "Enough is when we get this account of yours worked out."

So there I sat, with a hole in my new suit, as Tom wrote me out a year's worth of postdated checks. "Now Tom. I'll call you every month, a week ahead of depositing these checks, so neither of us has a surprise."

So, in the end, it all worked out - one less repo to take back to the dealer and a communication lesson for Mike.

SIX MONTHS LATER: GMAC FIELD MEETING

GMAC held quarterly field meetings at the Thunder Bird Hotel in Bloomington, Minnesota. This one was going to be fun because Mike had his own territory now, but, from time to time, we'd team up on tough repos. Everyone from management would be in attendance and we would be wined and dined because the excellent overall performance numbers. All the Field Reps were in attendance: Mark "Torch" Dunn, Kenny "Kobo" Knudsen, Woody Woodall, Jerome Masek, plus a host of other characters including our Branch Manager, Jim Everline. The waitress came around for the drinks order just before Jim Everline's opening remarks. Mike knew that Everline could be long winded, so he ordered three Vodka Gimlets right off the bat.

Jim Everline said, "Good afternoon gentlemen. Welcome to the Quarterly Field Meeting. The numbers are good, we still have some nagging problems, but I say, what is it if we can't have a little fun? You ask about promotions. I was a Field Rep in 1937. I was out in the field so long I thought we lost the war."

Jim Everline was followed by a host of boring people with boring reports, but this was the Field Reps party and we intended to drink and tell stories. And that we did.

THE END

P.S. It is February 28, 2006 and Mike McClellan and I haven't worked together since January 1980, but we've been in phone contact every week. We have a group of men called 'THE OVERACHIEVER'S CLUB' that meets monthly recalling the good old days.

ESCORTING THE QUEEN OF GENERAL MOTORS FRANCE

GENERAL MOTORS (GMAC) OFFICE, MINNEAPOLIS JUNE 1971

How could everything turn out so wrong? I had been the fair-haired Field Representative, then, after two years in the field, they promoted me to Credit Man. Big promotion - they took away my car and expense account and gave me a ten percent raise.

THE COMMUTE

I had built a new home in Brooklyn Park, which was located twenty-three miles from the General Motors office in Edina. I carpooled daily with three women from the office: Ann Williams, Fran Johnson, and Marsha Kloster. Ann and Fran drove in from Anoka, then the three of us picked up Marsha and her baby. We dropped the baby off at daycare before starting the twenty-three mile commute to work. At five p.m. we repeated the process in reverse, getting me home at six-thirty. During the entire ride the women would chitchat, but never did they talk about anything I was interested in. Turning up the radio wasn't effective in getting them to be quiet – it just made them talk louder. It was my easy-going nature that got me into this, but my steel determination would get me out.

THE JOB

"Slam! Bang!" Evelyn Kadermas slammed the ledger books down on her desk. Because she was located directly behind me, every time she slammed those books down, I jumped about a foot. You see, Evelyn was angry because, even though I was ten years younger than her, I was her boss and made more money. The big mistake that General Motors made was in their job titles. I was a 'Credit Man' and Evelyn was a 'Section Girl'. Just hearing those job titles gives me the creeps.

My desk partner was Fred Wallace. Together, Fred and I split twenty-five thousand accounts in our territory, which covered the State of Minnesota and Western Wisconsin. Our mission was to collect on accounts from the "current" category and never exceed four from the "sixty-day" category. There is no nice way to say this, but Fred Wallace was a total drunk. Every morning he'd show up hung over, looking like a walking dead man. I normally carried two sixty-day accounts, but Fred always had about fifteen or more. In addition to collecting, we had about eighteen Field Reps and District Reps to keep track of.

The office itself had about seventy people, about half of them smokers. Overall, the mood was very serious and the workload overwhelming.

THE QUEEN IS COMING

The Branch Manager, Jim Everline, called me into his office with a very worried look on his face. Mr. Everline had cause to be worried. He was a year from retiring and had taken to drinking heavily at lunch.

"Charlie," he said, "the wife of Philippe Belmont, Director of General Motors France, is flying into Minneapolis from Paris tomorrow. Mrs. Belmont will be accompanied by her ten-year old son, Johnny, and her mother-in-law, Esther. We'll meet them at the airport in a canary yellow Cadillac. Call Anderson Cadillac to make sure they have one ready for you to pick up this afternoon. Take Wallace with you to drive the other car, but you do all the talking. Now Charlie, I can't emphasize the importance of this assignment enough. Mrs. Belmont is a close friend of upper management and we need this done right."

"Yes sir, you can count on me, Mr. Everline. Everything handled correctly with respect."

I ran into the men's room, looked in the mirror and said to myself, "This is the best opportunity I'll get to be noticed by an important person. This is my big chance to be promoted to District Representative and get out of this noisy, smoky office."

One of the variables I needed to control was the appearance of Fred Wallace. I couldn't have him showing up all hung over and drab. I tapped Fred on the shoulder and said, "Fred let's go talk in the coffee room, I have a deal that I think you'll like."

When we had some coffee room privacy, I said, "Listen, this assignment tomorrow could be the best thing that's happened to me in a long time. I want, with all my heart, to make a favorable impression and I need just one thing from you."

"Now, what would that be Charlie?"

"I need you to look like you work for General Motors, not like a hung over car salesman."

"Oh yeah, Charlie? What are you going to do for me?"

"Well Fred, I'll work your sixty-day accounts and get your territory down to an acceptable level so they don't fire you. Does that sound like something that'll work for you?"

"Okay Charlie. Let me get this straight. I show up tomorrow, cleaned up and sober, and you'll work my sixty-day accounts and keep management off my back?"

"That's right."

"Charlie, you have a deal."

I called Bob Wuckerfenning at Anderson Cadillac to check on the canary yellow Cadillac. He said, "I'll have it ready in an hour. Yes Charlie, a real pretty Sedan Deville, canary yellow, just like you asked."

Fred Wallace dropped me off at Anderson Cadillac and I

left Ann Williams in charge of my car and the car pool. Yes, life was looking better already. Only, one day off the car pool and I'm driving a new Cadillac! My neighbors looked really surprised when I pulled into the driveway in that canary yellow Cadillac. I just told them I was on a secret company mission. That night I checked out my outfit – dark blue suit, light blue shirt, blue and red striped tie and black, wing-tip shoes. Yes, I was ready for 'Show Time'.

THE QUEEN ARRIVES

Mrs. Belmont and her party were due to arrive at the Minneapolis Airport at ten-thirty a.m., so I met Fred Wallace at the office at nine. When I saw Fred I was very relieved - he looked clear-eyed and all dressed up in a charcoal grey suit. I said, "Fred you look wonderful"

"Just don't forget our deal on the sixties."

"No Fred, a deal is a deal. I'll be on them as soon as we're done with the French contingent."

Judy Pint, the receptionist, said, "You guys look like your going to a wedding."

"No Judy, we're escorting the 'Queen of General Motors, France'."

The plane arrived at the gate. As the passengers deplaned, I instantly recognized the Belmont family because Europeans tend to dress more formally than Americans. We greeted them warmly and escorted them to the baggage claim area.

Mrs. Belmont introduced herself as Christine and her moth-er-in-law, Esther, and son, Johnny. I gave Christine a packet containing an oversized map of the area and my phone number in case of any problems. Then it hit me like a lighting bolt - the road to Highway 10 in Anoka was full of construc-tion zones. I said to Mrs. Belmont, "In view of the construc-tion zones, I'll drive you and your family to Anoka. It will just be easier."

"Well Mr. Blanchard, I appreciate your concern, but don't you have work to get back to?"

"I do, but my instructions are to do whatever is necessary to get you and your family safely to your destination."

"Then let's depart so we can get to the camp in Brainerd."

The ride to Anoka was very pleasant and I found the Bel-mont family to be kind and considerate. Poor old Fred was following me in the company mail car keeping a smile on his face as agreed. We arrived in Anoka about forty minutes later, right at the north end of town by Highway 10. "Well, this is the road to Brainerd. In three hours you should be at Camp Happy."

Esther said, "Excuse me young man, but we will be back on Tuesday, so book us into the St. Paul Hilton for three days and make it the best suite they have."

Christine nodded 'okay' and I said, "Consider it done."

That was the last I ever saw of the Belmont family.

On the ride back to the office, Fred was teasing me about all the catering to the needs of Christine Belmont. "I imagine, if the car broke down, you would've carried her, piggy back, to Brainerd."

"Yes I would have Fred. Piggy-back while pulling Esther and little Johnny in a Radio Flyer Coaster wagon."

"Well Charlie, let's head back and you can start helping me with my sixties and I can get management off my back."

"Yes Fred, I'll square both of us away and soon be promoted to District Representative."

THE QUEEN IS GONE, IT'S BACK TO HELL

August 1971

It was two long months and no one had heard from 'The Queen'. Didn't she know she was my lifeline in a stormy sea? Jim Everline, the Branch Manager, said, "No news is good news, Charlie."

"But Mr.Everline, she was just too classy not to call or write."

THE LETTER

I came walking into the office after a break and Jim Everline said, "Get Wallace and come in my office."

I grabbed Fred and we went to Jim's office. "Gentlemen," he said, " I just received a letter from Mrs. Belmont of Paris, France and, I think, we all know who that is. Mrs. Belmont sent the letter addressed to me through the president of

GMAC and the regional manager in Chicago. I'll give you both a copy, but I must read this one part: "The last thing our Johnny said before he went to sleep that first night in camp was, "Without Mr. Blanchard, we would never have made it to camp. I think I will say a prayer for Mr. Blanchard." God Charlie, you even got the kids praying for you."

TOUCHDOWN

On June 1, 1972 I was promoted to District Representative. "ALL HAIL THE QUEEN!"

THE END

Written: April 14, 2005

Escorting the Queen of General Motors France

THE GREAT CANADIAN GOOSE HUNT

G.M.A.C. OFFICE MAY 1971

The three of us were sitting in the coffee room at G.M.A.C office. From three very different backgrounds, we were the most unlikely hunting buddies you could imagine. I had grown up in Colby, Wisconsin, Woody had grown up in Thomaston, Georgia, and Mark was a city slicker who had grown up in Minneapolis, Minnesota. But, the one thing we had in common was hunting and fishing. All three of us spent most of our spare time doing it, preparing for it, or talking about it. This morning's topic of discussion was where our fall hunting trip would be. I thought we needed a full week in some remote spot for some good duck and goose hunting. "Look," I said, "Woody has a boat and trailer, I have a good Lab, and we can rent a travel trailer to stay in for the week."

Mark said, "That's all well and good, but where are we going to go?"

"Okay, I've done some research and I'll have it all together by tomorrow's break. I'll see you guys then."

NETLEY CREEK MARSHES
MANITOBA, CANADA

That night, I got all my hunting magazines together and pretty much put the whole hunting trip together. The next morning, at coffee break, I laid out my plan to Mark and Woody. I had an atlas with a map of Manitoba and showed the guys the hunting area known Netley Creek Marsh. They couldn't believe how big it was. Mark's first reaction was, "That's a long way to go, Charles, for a few ducks and geese."

I pointed out that this was one of the finest hunting areas in the world. "It may seem a little remote," I said, "but at least we won't have to put up with wall to wall hunters like we do back here in Minnesota. Guys, I got it all figured out, so let's see what you think." Then I laid out my plan. "We can use my company car to tow an eighteen foot trailer and put Woody's boat on top of the car. We can put our hunting equipment and clothes in the trunk and trailer."

Mark said, "Okay Charles, so far so good, but where is your dog, C.C., going to go or does he run along side the car all the way to Canada?"

"C.C. Rider will ride in a Kennel Aire Crate in the trailer and, when we stop for a pit stop, we let C.C. Rider out too."

Woody said, "What are we waiting for? Let's get the timed cleared with the boss and break the good news to our wives."

Yes that was one thing I hadn't thought of, we needed to

clear this with our wives.

THE CLEARING WEEKEND

Each of us had a simple assignment: to convince our spouses that spending nine days on a hunting trip was a worthwhile use of time. I had no fear because we had already gone on a winter vacation to Mexico. And Woody already had a deal in place: he'd agreed to move from Georgia to Minnesota if he could go hunting any time he wanted. That left Mark, who was a newlywed. But he was also a very good salesman. By Monday morning, all was well and all three of us had our clearances to proceed with the Great Canadian Goose Hunt.

NETLEY CREEK, MANITOBA,
THAT'S A LONG WAY FROM HERE

Yes, that's what my supervisor, Frank Brown, said, "Netley Creek, Manitoba. That's a long way from here. Do you realize its ten hours to Winnipeg and then another one hundred fifty miles west to Netley Creek?"

"Yes sir Frank, I mapped it all out and we should make it there in about thirteen hours.

"Don't forget, Charlie, you will be pulling a trailer and it will be hard to average fifty miles per hour."

"Well Frank, when you're on vacation, the clock doesn't

really matter, does it? We'll get there, when we get there."

"Vacation? You call that a vacation? Three guys sleeping in a little travel trailer - with a dog to boot? That's some vacation, Charlie, that's some vacation."

This kind of teasing did nothing but steel my resolve and make me want to go on the trip all the more. Sure, the average office jockey wouldn't drive thirteen hours pulling a trailer just to go goose hunting. But we weren't average office jockeys going on an average vacation close to home to have a mediocre experience. That's not what we were after; no, we were after an adventure - an experience to remember for the rest of our lives. And, as for "average", my Army Drill Sergeant once explained to me: "Average is the best of the worst and the worst of the best."

DUCK AND GOOSE SEASON DATES AND PRICES

I got on the phone and called John Schultz, G.M.A.C. Winnipeg, and found out that the duck and goose opener was October 12, 1971. John gave me some critical information: A non-resident license was $35, including the waterfowl stamp, and it was good for the season. Then I talked to a travel trailer dealer and found out we could rent an eighteen foot trailer for $8 a day. The only thing left to worry about was food and gas, but I figured we could probably do the whole trip for about $100 each. I reserved the travel trailer and told Woody and Mark that they should start thinking about what they wanted to eat. Woody said, "That's months away. Just put me down for beer and brats."

I knew the worst thing would be to get up there, miles from anywhere, and not have anything decent to eat. Yes, it would be very important to have good food with us, and, if I was going to be responsible for the food, I was going to make sure we were well prepared.

TRAINING THE RETRIEVER

I had bought a male Labrador pup a year and a half earlier from Cy Sifers of Cimaroc Kennels in Morris, Minnesota. Now, Cy was a super salesman who could sell a ice box to an Eskimo, but he hadn't exaggerated on this pup. I named the pup C.C. Rider and it wasn't long before C.C. was doing long water retrieves. I teamed up with my neighbor, Joe Campe, and Woody, and we trained three nights a week all summer long. Not only was C.C. a good retriever, but he was probably one of the prettiest dogs that I have ever seen. He had a thick, otter-like tail, a beautiful head, and weighed in at seventy-five pounds. The only thing I could fault C.C. for was that he had a stubborn streak and when he didn't want to do something, he would definitely let you know. But, all in all, C.C. was a great asset to the team and I couldn't wait to get him to Canada to retrieve those ducks and geese.

THE TRIP TO CANADA

The long awaited time had come. Early on a Saturday morning, we were all packed, loaded, and ready to go. We had the company car, a 1970 Chevrolet Impala, with a twelve-foot boat on top and an eighteen-foot travel trailer in tow. We set out at 3:00 a.m., intending to make it to Winnipeg, Manitoba by early afternoon. Our gear included five-horse-power Johnson outboard motor, twenty-four decoys, three shotguns, and ammunition. We put our suitcases, along with C.C. in his kennel, in the travel trailer and we were on our way. After we passed Fargo, North Dakota we hardly met a car until we got close to Winnipeg.

GO HOME UGLY AMERICAN

We arrived in Winnipeg and were driving down the highway looking for a McDonald's when we heard someone yell, "I hope you can shoot better than you can drive, you damn American."

I said to Woody, "What was that all about?"

"I don't know Charles, maybe they don't like your driving."

Finally, we spotted a McDonald's, so I pulled the car into the lot and parked in the back, so as not to block anybody. We walked in, ordered our food, and everything was fine until we laid our American Greenbacks down. At that moment, everybody in the restaurant figured out that we were Americans and all conversation stopped. We never did figure out why they hated us, but speculated that it was because of the 10% embargo on Canadian goods coming in to the United States. We hoped this wasn't a sign of things to come.

BASE CAMP

Our base camp was near a little town called MacGregor, about one hundred miles west of Winnipeg. On the way there, we stopped at Portage La Prairie to pick up some beer and liquor. Everything was about half the price it was in the United States because the Canadian dollar was only worth about sixty-five American cents. Maybe that's what the Canadians were so mad at Americans about. I wish I could have explained to them that we were just salaried workers trying to enjoy a little goose hunting and get away from "the man" for a week.

As we were driving, Woody said, "Look in the sky Charles, and tell me what you see."

I looked out across the prairie sky and all I could see for miles were the "V" formations of geese filling the sky. It was, and remains, one of the most incredible sights I have ever seen.

No one said a word, we just watched, in stunned amazement, one of the miracles of nature.

We parked the trailer in the space provided and were

pleased to find that we were the only people in camp. Thirty minutes later, we were all set up and ready to go hunting.

IGNORANCE OF THE LAW IS NOT A VALID DEFENSE

We drove up to the channel that was the lake entrance, hooked the motor up, and proceeded slowly for about a mile. The main reason we proceeded slowly was weight: Woody was six foot four, two hundred fifty pounds, Mark was five foot nine, one hundred sixty pounds, and I was five foot seven, one hundred eighty pounds. Plus we had a seventy-five pound dog, guns, and decoys all in a twelve-foot boat. This operation would work as long as we moved slowly through calm water, but if the situation changed, we'd all be swimming. As we edged into a likely spot, Mark said, "Here come the honkers."

And there they were, heading right for us, nice and low. We ducked, waited, and then, "Bang! Bang! Bang!" Three Canadian honkers fell into the water. C.C. was on the job and hit the water retrieving them one at a time. We stayed around for an hour and got some ducks, mostly Mallards, and a few Teal. It was starting to get dark, so we decided to head back because we didn't want miss the channel entrance. As we approached the docking area, we noticed two hunters who seemed to be waiting for us. As soon as we got out of the boat, they started chewing us out for using a motor on this part of the lake. We explained that we didn't know it was prohibited, but they replied, "Ignorance of the law is no excuse."

I apologized again and promised not to use the motor for the rest of the trip. The hunters walked away mumbling something about, "Damn American hunters."

THE MOUNTIES OR THE GREEN SHIRTS

The next morning, we were back at it. We left the motor behind, as promised, and rowing the boat, with all the guys and gear, was a tough job. We had been set up just about twenty minutes when, off in the distance, I spotted a green canoe with two men in it. I said, "Uh-oh boys, here come the game wardens."

Mark said, "How would you know that, Charles?"

"Well, it's like this. They're paddling that canoe almost effortlessly and way too even for a couple of hunters."

Sure enough, as the canoe got closer, we could see the green uniforms of the Canadian Department of Natural Resources.

"Okay guys, be very calm and very polite. This could be a minor chewing out or we could be in deep trouble."

One of the officers was an even-tempered Scotsman and the other was a hot-headed French Canadian. We owned up right away to the fact we had been using an outboard motor where it was forbidden. I leaned heavily on the fact that once the other hunters told us of our mistake we immediately took the outboard motor back to the camp. In the end, it was the Scotsman who agreed to let us off with a stern warning. Unfortunately, as a formality, he had to check our licenses and, as he reached to take my license, C.C. growled and showed his teeth. Immediately the French Canadian said, "See? They even have a vicious dog."

Fortunately, the Scotsman was a dog lover and he said, "No, he's just protecting his master."

We bid them a good day and thanked our lucky stars that we weren't on our way to jail.

THE WOMAN IN THE PURPLE DRESS

About mid-week we decided to venture into Portage LaPrairie, the biggest town in the area, to check out the bars. We found out quickly that Canada has some of the strangest drinking laws in the world. For instance, you can have a band playing in a bar, but no dancing is allowed unless the establishment has a dance license. You can't be served a drink at the bar and carry it over to a table yourself - you have to call a waitress over to move the drink. The three of us arrived at the local bar and went our separate ways: I ended up talking to a local drunk by the bowling machine, Mark was flirting with a beautiful woman in a purple dress, and Woody was at the other end of the bar. All of a sudden, a group of young men started circling Mark and me. I could see by their faces that they had enough of Mark flirting with their local beauty queen, so I quickly slipped over to get Woody. I told him, "It looks like a fight."

Woody said, "We don't want any trouble. We just came here for a good time."

"But your friends," a voice came from the crowd, "are smart asses."

Woody replied, "Yes, they can be and I apologize for them."

I don't know if it was Woody's diplomacy or his physical size, but the crowd backed off and we went home.

THE BEST DUCK HUNTING IS JUST BEFORE A STORM

It was the last day of the hunt and it seemed to be a perfect day for duck hunting. In other words, it was so rainy and nasty that you wouldn't want to do anything else. We headed out at about two in the afternoon, prepared to make the most of our last day. Things were pretty slow until an hour before dark when it seemed like the sky was raining ducks. C.C. was pretty much in a state of constant motion - retrieving ducks and turning right around again because two more had dropped. At fifteen minutes before dark, a storm blew in just as we were preparing to leave. The winds must have been blowing at about thirty to forty mile per hour and the waves were throwing the boat around like a bobber. Mark rowed and I pushed on his wrists to help him row. Woody says, "We're not getting anywhere. I have waders on, I'm going in to tow us."

Well everything would have been okay if the water hadn't been higher than Woody's waders. He soon became cold and tired and we finally convinced him to get back in the boat. I remembered that three shots was a distress call, so fired three shots, waited fifteen minutes, and then fired three more. Unfortunately, no one heard our distress signal, or no one cared, and we bobbed around the lake for another couple of hours. No matter how hard we tried, we couldn't find the channel to get back to the road. Finally, off in the distance, Woody spotted a light and took over rowing the boat. About a half hour later, three miserable hunters and one very wet dog tumbled onto to the porch of Alice Henderson. I explained our plight, but Alice was more interested in my last name than anything else. "Blanchard? Yes, there used to be a lot of Blanchards in this country. Any relatives up this way?"

Finally, Alice explained how to reach our car and we got back to base camp on the stroke of midnight. "Well boys," I said, "I have just enough chili for one more meal. Let me heat it up and we won't go to bed hungry." I turned on the stove and, in about two minutes, ran out of propane. The next morning we got up at 4:00 a.m., packed everything up, and headed home. Yes, home to house payments, jobs, and suburban living. If a vacation is defined as doing something completely different than you usually do, we definitely succeeded.

THE END

Written: February 20, 2007

A MAN CALLED P.W.

It was September of 1972 and I was feeling pretty cocky about being the youngest District Rep that GMAC ever had. I heard that a new health club was opening at the Radisson South in Bloomington. The club was called "THE EXECUTIVE CLUB'.

It was named that to lure all young wannabes who wanted to be thought of as

Executives. I walked in, joined up, and noticed a barbershop with a shoe sign stand just across the hall. I jumped in the chair and told the man, "Give me the best shine you got."

Just sitting there like that, I got a little stir crazy, so I asked the attendant his name.

"People call me P.W., but my name is Paul William Lawrence."

"Well that's a nice name. My name is Charlie and, if you're willing, I have a driving job for you tonight."

P.W. was a little skeptical and said, "Is it legal?"

"Well P.W., I'm a District Rep for GMAC and I need to move some cars around. I'll pay you ten bucks a car."

"That sounds good Charlie, but you have to pick me up since I don't own a car."

We became fast friends and during the next twenty-nine

years, P.W. Lawrence and I had a multitude of adventures. Following are a few of them.

P.W., PROFESSIONAL REPO DRIVER

P.W.'s pet name for me was "Chuck-O-Luck" and he always felt that it was important that I know the score.

"Now listen Chuck-O-Luck, there is no set of wheels I can't navigate. I used to haul cars for Ford Motor Company in Chicago and I was making $18,000 a year in 1953. Now, I got crossed up with the gal at the drug store and my wife divorced me, so now I shine shoes for a buck a pop. Take that as a life lesson: if you wink and she blinks, but she's not your wife, let it alone."

As we drove along, P.W. would continue his life lesson stories.

Our procedure was always the same: I'd call P.W. the night before to explain the situation. "Well, tomorrow we have to see Perry Kellerman on his 1978 Aspen. Now Perry is a professional wrestler. He's six foot nine and weighs four hundred pounds."

"Well holy friends of Jesus! How do you plan to deal with him Chuck-O-Luck?"

"I plan to be very tactful and see if we can work something out."

Perry lived in a trailer house five miles north of Anoka, which, in 1979, was the back woods or "the sticks", as P.W.

called it. All the way out to Perry Kellerman's place, P.W. read the notes and got more nervous by the minute.

"This man is huge Chuck-O-Luck. If he's mean, you're a dead man."

"Take it easy P.W., you can't tell a man's disposition by his physical description. We'll see how it is when we get there."

We arrived at Perry Kellerman's about nine thirty a.m., just as Perry was coming out of his house. He could barely fit through the door.

P.W. said, "That man will pick you up and crush you like a grape."

"Calm down P.W., I'm a trained man and I intend to get this worked out."

I introduced myself to Perry and he said, "Come on in, we'll talk about it."

P.W. looked scared as I walked into the house, but Perry seemed as meek as a lamb despite being as big as a bear. Perry poured his heart out to me explaining that he was abandoned on a hospital doorstep as a baby and that his adoptive parents were well off, but wanted him to make it on his own. Perry begged me not to take the car because then he wouldn't be able to get to his wrestling gigs.

"Hold on Perry. No one said I was repossessing any cars today. Let's see if we can work this out. You're ninety days past due, so I suggest a 90 day extension. The fee for this extension is $91.00, but I'll write it up as a hardship, so all

I need is a signature. In addition to that Perry, I need your word that, as soon as your folks get back, you'll sit down and set up a budget."

Perry stuck his hand out and shook mine saying, "Mr. Blanchard, you have my word on that."

When I walked out the door with the extension in hand, P.W. looked surprised that I was alive. "Well Chuck-O-Luck, you must be the luckiest man on earth to skate by that big dude."

"It's just a matter of how you approach people P.W. Remember to be kind at all times."

One of the most bizarre repo adventures I ever had with P.W. was the time we repossessed a fancy Dodge conversion van. The customer was Mitzi Brown and she worked at the Lee Lin Massage Parlor in Hopkins. The first time we tried to pick the car up at Mitzi's residence, she had a large Doberman chained to the front bumper. This set P.W. into a fit of laughter that I will never forget, he said, "Good thing they sent the dog trainer." P.W. was referring to my many years training Labradors.

Finally, we got lucky. We were cruising past the massage parlor and the van was sitting outside running. P.W. switched to the driver's seat of the company car we were in and sped up to the side of the van. I jumped out, rapped my fist on the door to make sure no Dobermans were about and then sped off to the repo lot. P.W. followed closely and, when we got to the lot, said, "Call the police and tell them, 'Mitzi Brown is now a pedestrian'."

I did call the police in case our repossession was reported as a theft. However, by the time I called the office, Mitzi was on her way in with the payoff in cash. I ran P.W. home and headed into the office to meet Mitzi. Once everything was paid, I delivered the van back to her residence. Mitzi's parting words were, "You didn't have to go through this trouble. We could have worked it out together."

I called P.W. and told him about Mitzi. He laughed and said, "What's on the docket for tomorrow?"

P.W.'S HERITAGE

P.W. lived in the black community, but was not really considered black by his neighbors. One day, on a long ride to South Dakota, he told me his story. His father was white and his mother was half African-American and half Comanche. Thus, P.W. had relatively straight hair, grey eyes, and light tan skin.

This genetic mix confused everybody and caused a lot of anxiety. One time, when P.W. was delivering cars in St. Louis, a dealer pulled him aside and said, "Just between you and me, what nationality are you?"

P.W. said, "Don't tell anyone, but I'm a Jap/Talian."

In the city, P.W. had no problem going into any restaurant, he was especially fond of Bob Peterson's Coffee Shop, but, when we were in rural areas, he'd insist on taking our food 'to go'.

"Well Chuck-O-Luck, you aren't prejudiced, so you don't think the rest of the world is either."

The race relation problem still troubles me, but P.W. taught me a lot.

P.W.'S BIRTHDAY PARTIES

P.W. told me once that his birthday was never celebrated very much in his life, even when he was a kid.

"Well P.W., that's all going to change because your 75th birthday is coming up on August 12, 1987, and we are going to celebrate."

"What we going to do Chuck-O-Luck?"

"Well, all the guys from Chrysler and GMAC, and Joanie too, are going to meet at Peterson's Coffee Shop to celebrate your birthday."

And party we did. P.W. even donned a party hat and we all sang 'Happy Birthday'.

P.W.'s birthday party became an annual event at Peterson's and the cast of attendees included all ages and backgrounds. Sally and Ralph Augustine even brought their girls, Hannah and Sarah, when they were five and three-years-old. One of the other guests was none other than F. Brian Forkey, a banker who wore two-thousand-dollar suits and five-hundred-dollar silk shirts. Well, Brian was sitting right next to three-year-old Sarah and was obviously very nervous about getting spilled on. I could see that P.W. was taking it all in and enjoying every minute of it.

After the party he said, "One little girl with a glass of milk intimidates the powerful banker."

P.W. had an uncanny ability to pick up on people's energy and analyze human moves.

Every year, as his birthday approached, it was all P.W. could talk about. He'd talk about who'd been there last year and who'd be there that year. The location, however, was un-changeable - it always had to be at Peterson's Coffee Shop. P.W.'s birthday parties went on until P.W. was in his late eighties and was just too frail to attend.

P.W. AND RELIGION

P.W. was a believer in God, but was very skeptical about organized religion. He once took a shine to a middle-aged woman who sang in the Baptist choir. Every Sunday, for ten Sundays in a row, P.W. dressed up in his Sunday best hoping to catch the attention of Earlene Braddock. Unfortunately, after all this effort Earlene was nothing more than polite.

P.W. called me and said, "I'm done with church and I hung up my church going clothes for good."

A few months later, Pastor Cassius Brown stopped by to see about P.W.'s physical and spiritual condition. "Now brother Paul, we have been missing you at Church and it is my duty as your Pastor to remind you come to Church and stay close to God."

P.W. retorted, "If God is everywhere like you say, then he is right here in my apartment and I don't need to go to church to be near him."

Pastor Brown bid his good-bye and P.W. never went to church again.

P.W., FISHERMAN

On all our travels P.W.'s favorite subject of conversation was fishing and how tired he was of fishing off the banks of local lakes in Minneapolis. A couple of years earlier, Joanie had rented a cabin at Bass Bay Resort in Osage, Minnesota and the fishing was pretty good. I called P.W. and suggested we go on a weekend 'Fishing Safari' and try our luck. I'd never seen P.W. get so excited. By the time the weekend came around, he had told his whole building the news. We got up to Osage and Bill Adams gave us a warm greeting and wished us good luck. We started fishing about seven p.m. and, by eight, we'd caught thirty-seven perch - all keepers. The next morning we caught thirty-five more, but then a storm moved in and ended our fishing for the weekend. On the ride back to town, P.W. must have said, "Oh my God, can we catch fish," about two hundred times. When P.W. started giving fish away to the women in his building, he became known as 'P.W., The King Of Fisherman'. Every time I'd stop by, one of the women would ask if I was P.W.'s fishing guide. I replied, "I certainly am and proud to be of service to such a fine man."

P.W. and I laughed about that for a week and people could think what they wanted. P.W. had both hips replaced in 1973 and as time went on, he was unable to get into a boat. P.W. said, "Well Chuck-O-Luck, you're going to have to be the whole package: fishing guide, fisherman, and fish cleaner."

"You bet P.W. I can do that and I will do that."

P.W., ASSISTANT DOG TRAINER

During the 1970s and 1980s I bought, sold, and trained retrievers for duck and pheasant hunters. The retrievers were mostly Labradors, with the occasional Golden and Chesapeake thrown into the mix. P.W. was my assistant trainer and buyer. This sideline had us traveling throughout Minnesota and the Dakotas.

One time, when I owned a female Labrador named "Double G Baby Snooks", I lined up a "romantic encounter" for her with a national field champion in Sioux Falls, South Dakota. I called P.W. to tell him about the rendezvous, and he said, "Sure I can make the trip. Let me call my good gal Margie to ride along."

When P.W. returned from South Dakota, he called and said, "Everything went fine except Snooky ate my turkey sandwich. I know that dog is a winner because when I was talking to Margie, she grabbed my sandwich."

Once, with P.W.'s help, I had a four-compartment dog trailer built and was pulling it with a 1968 VW Bug. We were breezing down the road to Albert Lea to pick up a couple of Yellow Lab pups, when P.W. looked down and saw that about four inches of snow had seeped in from floor boards.

"Chuck-O-Luck, we need a fancier ride."

So, I went out and bought a 1973 International pick-up. P.W. loved that truck. We put a topper on it and built in a dog equipment box for any and all training needs. Now, we could haul up to ten dogs and the equipment.

JANUARY 2001 - THE FINAL CALL

I had been calling P.W. for twenty-nine years, but on January 15, 2001 the phone had a funny ring and I got no answer - not even the machine. I drove over to his apartment, but the shades were pulled and it was locked down tight. I knocked on the door of P.W.'s next-door neighbor, Shirley Witherspoon. Shirley's husband answered and, before I had a chance to ask, said, "I'm sorry, your friend died yesterday."

"Do you know anything about the funeral arrangements?"

"No sir, but the family is here from Chicago and the funeral will probably be tomorrow."

I thought and thought, and then it came to me. If there were a funeral on the north side of Minneapolis, Estes Funeral would handle it. I called Estes and, sure enough, the funeral was at nine a.m. on Wednesday morning. I quickly called my lovely bride, Joanie, Tomas "Tommy" Rodriguez, and Glenn Schuster. I wanted to be rock steady for P.W. and everyone assured me they would be there – I knew I'd really need their support.

THE FUNERAL

I didn't know how P.W.'s family would receive me at the funeral, but things went well. When I walked in, his younger sister, Odessa, called out, "You must be Chuck. In fact, I think my brother called you 'Chuck-O-Luck'."

I replied, "One in the same. This is my wife, Joan, and our good friend, Tommy Rodriguez."

Glenn Schuster arrived later and the four of us sat together on the right side and P.W.'s family sat on the left. I looked at Tommy and said, "Will segregation ever die?"

P.W.'s people were churchgoers who considered P.W. a drinker and a heathen. The family was there to put him to rest, but certainly not to honor him. I mingled as much as I could and met his thirty-seven year-old daughter, Robin. I mentioned that I was there when P.W. received her high school graduation announcement and how excited he was. Robin replied, "He could have at least called or sent a card."

Yes, I could see that a tone of resentment pervaded the room. I scanned the room, but none of P.W.'s former girl-friends were there. Neither Catherine nor the ever steady,

Margie, showed up for P.W.'s last call. Then I looked up and a smiling young woman came towards me. It was none other than Terri Simmons, Catherine's and, I believe, P.W.'s, daughter. We talked briefly and I could see the pain in her eyes of losing her father.

The preacher was a six-foot-four, African-American man who delivered a great eulogy and brought the congregation to its feet. Yes, the Reverend Caleb Jones was born to do this work and he certainly delivered for P.W. on that day. Then came the time in the service when the family was asked to speak some words about P.W., but no member of the family came forward. I volunteered and walked up front, with my heart in my throat, hoping I could come up with a few good lines. I actually don't remember my eulogy very well, but I do remember saying, "P.W. was like a father to me. He was a good friend through good times and bad."

The burial was at Fort Snelling National Cemetery and as they were shooting the three gun salute, I remembered P.W.'s last words to me, "We're just a couple of ex-GIs, Chuck-O-Luck. We will do well wherever we go."

THE END

THE RELUCTANT COACHES

MINNESOTA TRUCK CENTER
APRIL 1980

Well, I had finally landed the job I wanted and, after a couple years of skillful negotiation, it was starting to pay off. Previously, I had worked for Chrysler Credit and found out during a truck audit that the credit manager at Minnesota Truck Center was Vic Olson - one of my former bosses at GMAC. And, to top it all off, the owner of Minnesota Truck Center was also a former GMAC manager. I stopped in at the truck center whenever it was convenient and, finally, Vic said, "Come in on the first of the year. You can have my job, I'm retiring."

After a few interviews with the owner, Don Bergthold, I started with a forty percent increase in pay and a promise of an incentive plan that would pay even more. I handled all the credit approval, but the bulk of the collections work was handled by the office staff, which consisted of ten women. These women were the key to my success and I did everything I could to keep them happy, including buying lunches, incentive plans, and buying flowers.

WE NEED A COACH

One day, my top producer, Susie Kocchenerger, leaned over and said to me, "Will you be our coach?"

"What kind of coach?" I asked

"I belong to a women's softball league and we have a woman coach now, but even she admits she is terrible."

I didn't pause one second, even though I had never coached even a men's team. I said, "I certainly will."

MEETING THE WOMENS SOFTBALL TEAM

Now, in 1980, women's softball was just coming into its own, but my team was a typical team of the 1970s. We had one person who had the makings of a pitcher; our outfielders were pathetic - they couldn't catch a fly ball to save their lives; and the coach, Betty Lee, had made herself shortstop, but she couldn't throw or catch. I held my practice and then we had a team meeting. I offered my observations on the team's future. Basically, I told them we had a long way to go and I would like to introduce some younger players to the team, thus some of the regulars would be playing halftime. Furthermore, I explained, "If I'm going to take on the job as coach, I am totally in charge."

Well, you could cut the tension with a knife, but when I asked for as show of hands the majority voted for me to be coach.

COACHING IS NOT A ONE MAN JOB

Coaching is not a one-man job. So, to survive in this world you must have friends. I got on the phone and called my two good buddies from Chrysler, Rich Roeder and Glenn Schuster. Both Glenn and Rich were single and probably wouldn't mind being around some pretty girls. And I knew if I asked them anything, that they would help me. Both were on board and they said they would meet me at practice. The practice went okay, but Rich said we had a lot of players who are here to be social, but don't have the skills to play ball.

"Yes, we have a lot of work to do to make this group into a team." I replied

"Well we will soon because we have a game next week."

All that night I couldn't sleep and I wondered what I could do to help the team.

FIRST GAME - A NIGHTMARE WAITING TO HAPPEN

I could tell it would be a night to remember when I watched the other team take the field. I mean, the other team looked like athletes and our team looked like their over-the-hill relatives. In the first inning, our shortstop made four errors, I substituted Kathy, and, a moment later, the former shortstop was running off with the equipment bag. Glenn caught up with her and I tried to reason with her, but she just sat on the bench crying. The final score was 17 to 0 and I wondered what I had gotten the boys into. The rest of the season was more of the same and some of the older players said they would like to play half a game and I should recruit some new players. I talked it over with Glenn and Rich and we agreed we needed a pitcher, a shortstop, and second base that could hit. It was time to go recruiting.

SOMETIMES TREASURES ARE HIDDEN IN THE ODDEST PLACES

I was bartending part-time at Roy's Tavern and the person I split the job with was none other than Debby Anderson. Debby Anderson was nineteen and had been the top softball player at Fridley High School. I explained my dilemma and she said, "I can get my neighbor, Leslie Goode, she's seventeen, and one of the top players in the state. Oh, by the way Chuck, she doesn't drive, so you'll have to get her to games and practice."

"No problem. Tell Leslie she has a driver now."

The next night I had a date with my girlfriend, Joan, and told her about my recruiting problem. Joan said, "Ask my daughter, Linda, she's a very good athlete and knows all kinds of people."

Linda came walking in and I said to myself, "That's my new pitcher."

Meanwhile, back at the truck center business, was booming and all the women in the office were happy. I was getting checks so big, I thought they had the wrong guy. So, if all it took was a little coaching then so be it.

NEW TEAM ON THE HORIZION

The team struggled through that first year and I never would have lasted if it wasn't for Rich and Glenn. Those guys were at every game - Glenn handling the statistics and Rich coaching first. We had learned a lot from our first year, mostly that we needed new players. Well, I went recruiting and had some the new players. We now had Deb Anderson at shortstop. Deb was twenty years old and had been a stand-out player at Fridley High. Leslie Good at third base. Leslie was 17 and one of the top high school players in the state. Linda Breen was our new pitcher. I'd practiced with Linda several times. She would be a good pitcher and was good at bat. Linda enlisted her friend, Barb, "Peaches", and we had a new catcher. We would see what the season brought, but we were looking more like a completive team every day.

LINDA BREEN SHINES AS PITCHER AND TEAM REACHES PLAYOFFS

What a difference a year makes. The personnel chang-es helped. Last year's Dave's Bar women's softball team was not taken very seriously, but now or opponents feared us. And we were in the playoffs. Linda was batting about 400 and holding the opponents to two points per game with her deadeye pitching. With Deb and Leslie batting second and third, you could hear the bat cracking and see them fly around the bases. And what can we say about "Peaches"? She was rock steady as the catcher and a great support to Linda. The rest of the team responded in kind to this young talent, and we had a competitive team.

THE PLAYOFFS - EVERYONE WANTS TO TAKE CREDIT

Well, last year no one paid attention to us, but this year everyone showed up to watch us in the playoffs. I mean everybody – husbands, old boyfriends, new boyfriends, but I was expecting this new fondness to go away. The best thing for me was to stick to my game plan and ignore these new found fans. I told Linda, "Get in the zone. Let's keep this a low scoring game."

I told the rest of the team, "Hit and run hard. If we get tagged out once too often, that's okay. We want aggressive base running."

THE FINALS

"Crack!" went the bat. Leslie had just hit a homerun to tie the game at three and we have two outs. Deb Anderson, uncharacteristically, popped out and the opposing Cardinals were up for their last at bat. I was looking at Diane, who had been sitting on the bench all year and decided to substitute her for Rachel in center field. Big mistake. On the first pitch the Cardinals hit a homerun and won the game. To the credit of the players, no one harped on me for the decision that lost the game.

THE COACHES TAKE A HOLIDAY

Well, the season was over and the reluctant coaches, Rich Roeder, Glenn Shuster, and Chuck Blanchard, decided to take a road trip to Milwaukee. I planned it all and take full credit for sitting on my billfold, to the detriment of the trip, which ended up being very boring. We got permission to use Glenn's company car to save on transportation costs and it was my dumb idea to stay at the YMCA. We arrived at the Y, got settled, then, at about three, there was a knock on the door. The YMCA attendant told us that he was there to fumigate the room. Well, Rich being the fastidious fellow that he was, freaked out and told me, "Let's check out." I calmed Rich down and we proceeded to the Brewers game. After the game, we went to the Fish Fry to visit with my Uncle Russell. Later that night, we checked out Rockie's Bar, but everything was pretty dead. The only excitement was a sighting of Doc Severinsen jogging at the Y. Well, I sure didn't treat my coaches to a very good time. I told to Glenn, "Maybe we'll do it next year, maybe we won't. Put this Chrysler in gear, let's head home."

JUNE 27, 2010

A SAD DAY FOR ALL ATHELETES

Rich Roeder died at age 74. He'd been a friend of mine since 1976 and was always there when I needed him. He was a father, little league coach, but he was most well known as a distance runner. Rich completed more than 750 long distance races, including many marathons.

THE END

Written: January 9, 2011

MY MARATHON CAREER

I have always had a fascination with running. But, truth be told, my real strength is sprinting, not long distance running. Be that as it may, I'd always wanted to run a marathon. And, from 1983 to 1989, I finally did. I ran Grandma's Marathon in Duluth, Minnesota, The New York Marathon in New York, New York, and The London Marathon in London, England. Following is a detailed account of my preparation and running of these three marathons.

GRANDMA'S MARATHON: DULUTH, MN
JUNE 11, 1983

I started my training regimen in January 1983. Which was, basically, to see if I could jog five miles every day. Let's just say my life style at the time was not conducive to a full fledged training regimen: I spent three nights a week with my girlfriend, Joan Breen, and three nights at the Shorewood, leaving only one day to train. I was a regular at the Shorewood Inn in Fridley, and my nickname was 'Good Time Charlie'. The regulars at the Shorewood were simply amazed that, at the age of 38, I would even attempt to run a marathon.

Slowly but surely the months passed, my "training" continued, and everyone around me was sure that I would chicken out. But I was determined. If I had to run, crawl, or walk, I was going to run, and finish, Grandma's Marathon. Race day loomed. My training regimen had not improved much, but you have to do what you have to do. Joan secured a place to stay from a friend, Sharon Lund, and, when we met, I could see the surprise in Sharon's eyes. She must have been thinking, "This guy is going to run a marathon?"

RACE DAY: TWO HARBORS, MN
JUNE 22, 1983

All of us 7,000 plus marathon types assembled in Two Harbors. We would be running twenty-six miles, three hundred eighty-five yards, along Lake Superior to Duluth. As I was standing in line, the race officials lead a runner from Kenya to the head of the pack. I remarked to a fellow runner, "Now that's the body type a guy needs to win marathons." The other runner agreed, but doubted if either of us ever would.

"Bang!" The starting gun went off and I was officially running my first marathon. I was feeling pretty good and, after a mile or so, I started running with a guy and two gals. They were in their early thirties and introduced themselves as Tom, Stacy, and Kelly. We were cruising along and when we passed the eight mile mark, there was Joan waving. I assured her that everything was going good and we continued to roll along with Kelly setting a brilliant pace. Then the sun came out. It got hotter and hotter until, at mile sixteen, my body said, "No! I can't take anymore!"

Kelly said, "We can't just leave you."

"Run your race. I'll make it one way or another," I replied.

I was coming up on mile eighteen. The sun was scorching and my legs were aching big time. There was no relief in sight and I wouldn't hit the shade trees until mile twenty. Finally, at the north end of Duluth, I hit mile twenty. The shade of the trees felt great, my legs felt a little better, but still all I could manage was a half trot. It was going to be a long day, but quitting was not on my mind.

When I was within one mile of the finish line, the theme song from 'Rocky' started playing in my head, and I began to pick up speed. Then I heard my old drill instructor, Sergeant Porter, talking, "Blanchard, you can't march but you sure can run." I hit the one hundred yard mark and started sprinting. I sprinted right to the end and into the arms of my beloved Joan. My time was a terrible five hours twenty nine minutes, but I didn't care. I did it! The kid from Colby ran a marathon. Joan told me that the hospital tents were full of runners and that she had been worried. I said, "Stick with me baby. With a little luck, you'll be wearing diamond bracelets or handcuffs."

NEW YORK MARATHON: NEW YORK, NY
NOVEMBER 1, 1987

So, I'm sitting at work and this thought comes to me: if I skip lunches for the next six months, I can afford to run the New York Marathon. I ran over to Joan's house and told her my plan, to which she replied, "Skip supper too and take me with you."

"Okay then. I'll book us a room at The Empire Hotel and start training."

My training regimen had changed drastically for the better since Grandma's Marathon. The government had strongly suggested that I change my lifestyle (a story for another time) and 'Good Time Charlie' went into retirement. My old training regimen of three nights with Joan, three nights at the Shorewood, and one night training changed to: three nights with Joan, three nights training, and one night at the Shorewood drinking Coca-Cola. Yes, I certainly would be in better shape for this marathon than I had been for Grandma's. I was down twenty-five pounds and running thirty-five miles a week.

We arrived at the Empire Hotel, which is located directly across from the Lincoln Center, on the Upper East Side of Manhattan. I had stayed there for a month in 1985 and the place held a lot of fond memories. Joan was pumped up just at the idea of being together in New York again.

Runner registration was at the Sheraton ten blocks away,

so away we went. I was handed a race map and told that buses would start transporting runners to Staten Island at 5:00 a.m. The marathon started on Staten Island, went north through Brooklyn, Queens, and the Bronx, then finished in Central Park in Manhattan.

RACE DAY

It's race day and Joan and I are up at 4:00 a.m. because I need to catch the bus to Staten Island at 5:00. As we near the area where the buses are loading, we see tons of people, both runners and the people who are seeing them off. Joan kisses me goodbye and I'm off to find my bus. As I approach the bus, I notice an Italian couple in an intense discussion with their daughter, who is the runner. The father motions to me to come over, "You're the one," he say, "you're the right guy for the job."

He continues, "Hello sir, my name is Al Martinelli. This is my wife, Gina, and my daughter, Angelina."

"Well Al, my name is Charlie. How can I help you?"

Al was about five feet four and his wife and daughter were about five feet eight, but Al was definitely in charge.

"You see Charlie, we need someone to escort our Angel to see she gets breakfast and gets to the right starting place. And we know if she doesn't appear to be alone, no one will bother her."

"I'm your man, Al. I would be glad to escort Angel, but

what does Angel think?"

Angel spoke right up and said, "Whatever Daddy says is fine with me."

"Well, let's go Angel. We have a marathon to run."

Al said, "Just a minute Charlie, I want to give you some money."

"No Al, this one's on me. I can't take money for doing a good deed."

Al hugged me. Gina hugged me. Angel hugged her parents. And then, finally, Angel and I got on the bus and were off to Staten Island. The 1987 New York Marathon had twenty-two thousand runners and, with all those people, I made sure that Angel got to the right spots. We went to a stretching class led by Swedish runners and then to get our bagels and tea. Race time was 8:00 a.m. and Angel and I started to line up at 7:00. "KAABOOM!" The cannon went off and this great mass of people started slowly moving forward. Runners settled into their comfortable paces and, at about the four mile mark, people were starting to put distance between each other. Angel winked at me and said, "Thanks a bunch. I gotta get going."

Yes, Angel had to run her race. The last I saw of her were her pigtails bouncing, finding her own pace, and leaving me to find mine.

Joan had read the subway map the night before and planned to track me along the route. At about the eight mile mark, I looked over and there she was, so I stopped momentarily to give her a kiss. A young man from the crowd remarked, "I seen that!"

The kiss and the remark bolstered my spirits.

The race was going along fine and Joan was supposed to meet me at the sixteen mile mark, but I found out later she had just missed me. The New York crowd was wonderful – they shouted encouragement and handed out slices of oranges and apples to help the runners avoid dehydration. I came across a bridge, not sure where I was, and a young man with a brandy bottle said, "Welcome to the Bronx."

I was running well into Harlem and approaching mile twenty-four when I noticed a man about fifty-five running so slow he was almost walking. I pulled up alongside him and noticed a '1ST AIR CAV' tattoo on his arm. I said, "Hey soldier, you having troubles?"

"Yes, I don't think I'll make it."

We introduced ourselves, his name was Joe from Cleveland and his running party had left him behind. "Listen Joe, I'm ahead of schedule and am going run with you to the one hundred yard mark. That's where I sprint in."

So run together we did. Running quick for one block, then coasting the next. At the one hundred yard mark, Joan was waiting, intending to race to the end with me and get a picture. I dug in, sprinted, and finished the race at 4:29. Joan, laughing, finally caught up to me - in her mind, she'd thought she could beat me and still have time to take a picture.

NEW YORK MARATHON CELEBRATION

I have never had a more magical night than the one in New York at the after marathon celebration. Joan and I changed clothes and went to the Carnegie Deli for pastrami sandwiches and a little New York Cheese Cake. I put my marathon medal on and we walked, with maybe a little strutting on my part, down Broadway. Strangers offered congratulations and at the deli, people got up from their tables to come over and shake my hand. A elderly lady named Martha asked if she could sit with us and just hear about the marathon. We told our story and Martha told about working in an office for fifty years. Oh yes, it was a magical night long to be remembered.

LONDON MARATHON: LONDON, ENGLAND
APRIL 23, 1989

I had been planning to run the London Marathon ever since I completed the New York Marathon, but circumstances had changed. You see, on January 1, 1989, Joan Breen and I split up. I would be getting ready for this marathon without my life coach, my friend, and my lover. So, I put all my focus into getting ready for London and tried not to dwell on my love life problems.

A friend of mine, Paul Martella, got me a free ticket to Tampa, Florida, so during the first week of January, 1989, I ran ten miles a day on the beaches. I flew back to cold Minnesota to continue my training for the April marathon.

During the months leading up to the marathon, I threw all my energy into training. My work schedule was such that I worked late two days a week. On Mondays and Wednesdays, I got up at five a.m. to run eight miles. On Tuesdays, Thursdays, and Fridays, I ran five miles after work. On weekends, I generally ran a ten miler. I shed another twenty pounds and my mother thought I was down three suit sizes.

On April 21, 1989 at 2:30 p.m., I boarded the plane to London. I arrived, completely jetlagged, in London at 8:30 the following morning. Joan had given me the name of a reasonable bed and breakfast, but I arrived too early to check in. The host said I could leave my luggage, go get checked in for the marathon, and come back to check in. Good plan, but after I checked in at marathon central and returned to the bed and breakfast, my luggage was missing. My heart sank as I wondered what I was going to do without my running shoes and the rest of my clothes. The B & B manager said, "Do not worry sir, when they get to the airport, they will realize their error, and have your luggage sent back. I suggest you go to your room and rest for the marathon. We will call you when your luggage arrives."

How he could be so confident was beyond me, but I went to my room and tried to sleep. About two hours later the manager knocked, "Sir, your luggage has arrived."

I jumped out of bed and ran to the door. "Not to worry,

Sir," he said, "most people want to do the right thing."

I took the Tube (London's subway) to the start of the race at Black Heath Park, then lined up with the other runners who, like me, expected to finish in the four hour range. As I approached some Englishmen one of them said, "Good morning, Sir."

"Good Morning," I replied and offered that I was an American.

"Obviously you are sir. And what state are you from?"

"I am from the great State of Minnesota, home of Dick Beardsley, who ran a two minute, nine second marathon here last year."

"Oh. Well sir, we all know who Mr. Beardsley is. Do you plan on emulating his performance?"

"No sir, I just plan to run the best race I can."

The London Marathon course starts at Black Heath, loops through Greenwich, past the Cuttysark, and across Tower Bridge. Circling Canary Wharf, the course runs along the Thames, past the Tower of London, through Trafalgar Square, and onto the Mall, where it finishes in front of Buckingham Palace. On this crisp April day, a total of forty-four thousand runners were entered and a crowd of spectators over a million strong was expected to cheer us on.

The race was on and, slowly but surely, this gang of forty-four thousand runners inched forward and I was feeling about as good as a man could feel. The only thing missing was Joan at the eight and sixteen mile marks, and, of course, at the finish. But nothing could be done about that, and I needed to concentrate on my pace. In Europe, many countries run in teams and carry banners from their local town. I was fortunate enough to run along with an Irish team and the race seemed to breeze by with all the drinking songs. Mile eight came and went and it was on to mile sixteen and then mile twenty four. I was well under my four hour pace and then it happened. It felt like someone shot me in the left calf. I pulled over and my calf muscle had retracted - it looked like a flat tire. Fortunately for me, two young nurses came to my aid and one of them said, "Don't worry, it's just a cramp."

They massaged my calf and I was back on the road in six minutes. I stutter-stepped the next two miles and then it hit me: my drill instructor was in my head saying, "Blanchard, we always finish our races with a sprint." So I dug deep and started passing people. When I hit the finish line, the time was four hours nine minutes - my best time ever.

POST MARATHON TRIP

After the race, I took a week long trip to Northern England and Scotland. My fondest memory is staying with Hugh and Moira White in Ayre, Scotland. Before I had left for the marathon, Joan had recommended the White's Bed & Breakfast. I stayed with them for three days and must have told stories eight hours a day. Hugh was an electrical engineer and Moira was a surgical nurse. They had a daughter nicknamed 'the wee lass' and a large Labrador named Honey. When my vacation was over and it came time to go I said, "I need to settle up with you on my bill."

Hugh said, "We could never charge you because you have entertained us for three days."

I gave everyone a sincere thank you and was on my way.

THE END

P.S. Joan and I worked it out and were married June 10, 1999. I will always remember the marathons.

My Marathon Career

RITCHIE'S BAR

8TH STREET AND 3RD AVENUE, MINNEAPOLIS, MN
DECEMBER 1975

I was working as a Field Representative for Chrysler Credit doing field collections and conducting dealer audits when Bob Peterson called. Bob had trained me in at Embers Restaurants back in 1965 and we had been friends ever since.

"Listen Charlie. Remember Riva Nelson? She has a restaurant connected to Ritchie's Bar and I'm thinking of taking over the spot. Let's stop in today, see how her business is, and then stop back tonight and see how Ritchie's Bar is doing."

"That sounds good to me." I replied. "I'll meet you at Riva's Café at 1:15 tomorrow."

RIVA NELSON A LEGEND IN HER OWN MIND

Both Bob and I knew Riva very well because we'd worked with her when she was a waitress at the Guest House Embers. Now she was the hostess, waitress, and cook all rolled into one in this one-woman show. She took our order and then chewed us out for not ordering something more expensive so she could make a little money. When we were ready to go, she asked if we would take her miniature poodle for a trim and she would give us a dollar. Riva had survived the Russian Displaced Person Camp and she would use any one she could as long as it served her purpose. We were glad to leave with no assignments, vowing never to go back as long as Riva was there. But, while I was fretting over how ungrateful Riva was, Bob was smiling from ear to ear.

"You know Charlie, her place would work if I get the right people in there. With my menu, it would really work - especially with all the people to draw from downtown. I just have to make my deal with Ritchie and this will be a great place to have 'Peterson's Coffee Shop'."

RITCHIE'S BAR, RITCHIE KOVAL, PROPREITOR

Bob had warned me that Ritchie could be a little gruff, but he was enough to scare a person straight. Ritchie Koval was six-foot-three and about two hundred and thirty pounds. He had an Army drill instructor's haircut and wore a white shirt and starched khaki pants. Clearly this man had spent some time in the Army. And when he talked and laughed, you could hear him a half block away.

Ritchie kept a very clean bar and expected his patrons to treat his place in a very respectful way. Woe to the man who came into the bar and put his cigarette out on the floor. Once, I observed a customer talking wildly - waving his hands and grinding his cigarette out on Ritchie's perfectly waxed floor. Ritchie went right over the bar and said, "What the Hell? Do you do that at home?"

The man didn't have a chance to answer. Ritchie picked him up by his belt and shoved him out onto the street. Another man made the mistake of putting his cigarette out in the men's room urinal. Ritchie calmly picked the cigarette up with a tweezers and put it in the mans drink saying, "You forgot something didn't you?"

So, if you were a regular, you abided by the rules knowing that if you didn't abide by the rules, you weren't a regular for very long.

RITCHIE'S BAR HOURS OF OPERATION

It's a pretty safe bet that no other bar anywhere had the same hours of operation that Ritchie's did. Basically, he posted that the bar was open for business from 11:00 a.m. until 6:00 p.m., Monday through Friday with no weekend hours. The catch was, if he knew you and liked you, the buzzer at the back door could be hit and you would walk into a full bar. Actually, Ritchie's was Campbell Mithun's private club - on any given night after 6:00, you could look down the bar and see George, the Art Director, shaking a dice game, usually Six Five Four, for quarters. These games would go on until about 9:00 and then Ritchie would give everyone a look and everybody would clear out. Most of the time, Ritchie would tell everyone to drive safely and give a call once they got home.

THE CAST OF CHARACTERS
SARGE

Now, I don't think anybody ever knew Sarge's real name. What we did know was that Sarge was a security guard who had retired from the Army after thirty years of service. Sarge rented a sleeping room at a hotel next door to Ritchie's and would come into the bar at 4:00 p.m. and stay until Ritchie told him it was time to go home. One of Ritchie's pet peeves was that Sarge would get drunk while still wearing his gun belt. Eventually, Sarge agreed to take his gun home first and then start drinking.

One morning, after a very tough night, Sarge came in and plopped himself on the bar stool. Richie came by with a manila envelope and emptied the contents on the bar. "Sarge," Richie said, "you left $147.60 on the bar last night. Straighten up and fly right."

A very embarrassed Sarge picked up his money and went home.

GEORGE NELSON, ART DIRECTOR, CAMPBELL MITHUN ADVERTISING

No one in the world could dislike George Nelson because

he didn't have a mean bone in his body. George dreamed of having his own cabin on the lake where he could fish for walleyes. Every night he would say, "Ritchie, by this time next year I'll be up at my lake cabin, living off the fat of the land."

Ritchie would laugh and say, "George, for what you spend on booze, you could have bought ten cabins."

"Well, what can I say, a man can dream can't he?"

Yes, George enjoyed that Richie was a little skeptical and he liked to trade a little banter.

DON CASTLEMAN, PBX REPAIRMAN

Don Castleman worked for Bell Telephone as a PBX repairman at all the big offices downtown. Don believed in taking the bus everywhere, so, on the nights I stopped in, I would give him a ride home. Not that Don cared about riding the bus. I hate buses and always figured that, if a man has worked thirty years for the same company, he shouldn't have to ride a bus. For a number of years Don and I were hunting partners and he showed me some secret grouse spots up near Mora.

I've always liked voices and Don had a crystal clear voice with a crisp delivery. He also had a great memory and would deliver a synopsis of the news everyday at Ritchie's Bar. Don loved the name, 'Richard Millhouse Nixon', and when he would greet me he would say, "Hello Charles Millhouse. How are you?"

NO FLIRTING WITH THE LADIES IF YOU'RE MARRIED

Occasionally, since Ritchie's Bar was right downtown, a young woman would wander in for a drink. This, of course, delighted all the male patrons and everybody would be on their best behavior. However, if Ritchie caught one of his married patrons flirting, he would find a way to stifle the action. A group of pipe fitters used to stop in once in a while and each one of them thought he was the greatest lady's man that ever lived. One day, an attractive brunette stopped in and sat right next to Brian Nitty. You could just see Brian swell with pride as he told of his many accomplishments and all the dangers of the job. The brunette looked like she was very interested in continuing the conversation elsewhere, then Ritchie caught the action. No way did he want his bar known as a pick-up joint, so off he went to stifle the shenanigans. He said to Brian, "Hey, your wife just called and she wants you to bring home a quart of milk for the baby."

And then he looked at the brunette and said, "You're not a home wrecker are you?'

Brian sulked and the brunette picked up her purse and left.

RITCHIE'S ATM MACHINE...BEFORE ATMS WERE INVENTED

In the mid 1970s ATMs were unheard of, so, what did you do if you needed some extra cash to go drinking? Well, thirst no more. Just drive down to Ritchie's Bar and hit the buzzer on the back door. Two hits on the buzzer and the door would burst open and Ritchie would yell, "Hey Kid, what you doing?"

"Well Ritchie, I need to cash a check."

"No problem kid, come on in."

Then Ritchie would quiz you as to which bars you were going to hit and ask that you call him when you got home. You see, Ritchie really didn't want to go with you, he just liked to live vicariously through his customers.

THE CHAMPAGNE BREAKFAST
JUNE 1978

All the predictions came true for Bob Peterson's Coffee Shop. Your average downtown diner had never seen such a variety of pancakes and omelets. Bob went from a one cook, one waitress operation to a hostess, three cooks, three waitresses, and a dishwasher. The total seating capacity for Peterson's Coffee Shop, including Ritchie's Bar, was ninety people. And would you believe, that even with a seating capacity of ninety, some days Bob would serve over five hundred people. But Bob was still looking for higher hills to climb, so he proposed to me that we should have a Champagne Breakfast. I said, "That's fine, but what does have to do with me?"

"Well Charlie, we need a great bartender who can serve the people and keep them coming back for more. Now Charlie, I think you're our man, but you have to convince Ritchie that we can handle his bar while he is gone for the weekend."

I had a long talk with Ritchie and explained that I would be sure to keep a lid on things and the place would be as clean as he left it. I did add that, to be sure I wasn't influenced by the crowd, I would not drink myself while I was tending bar. That did it. Ritchie could see that I was serious and he gave the go ahead for the Champagne Breakfast. "Now, as far as you pay goes," Ritchie said, "I will give you 15% of the gross and you keep all your tips."

This was more than generous and I'm glad Ritchie came up with it because I would have worked for much less. Okay, we were all set, all we had to do was promote the event a little bit.

During the following week, Bob put up a sign in the restaurant promoting the Champagne Breakfast on Saturday. The restaurant was chugging along at full speed, serving over five hundred people some days. That meant, with a seating capacity of ninety, he was turning over the full capacity of the restaurant five times in a eight hour period. This was a great compliment to the hard-working staff that cooked and served the well-planned menu.

The bar opened up for the Champagne Breakfast at eight a.m. and I was there an hour ahead of time to have breakfast. Bob's crew was already there: Kathy McNair was the hostess, making sure everyone got to the right spot; Bob's wife, Linda, Betty Lou, and Annie were all ready to serve the food; and, along with Bob, Charlie and Joe were cooking. So, a seasoned crew was ready to go.

There was a steady stream of customers all morning and it stayed steady until about one p.m. Then, at 2 p.m., Bob locked the door on the restaurant, but I didn't lock the door on the bar. The remaining crowd of about thirty people came into the bar and we partied until one a.m. the next morning. I mean, the jukebox was jumping and Judy Christensen, who used to work with Bob and I at Embers, was dancing on the bar. Finally, Bob and I got everybody out the door before and then we had to clean up. It took us about an hour and a half, but, when we were finished, the bar was spotless. Yes, this was probably the best revenue day for Ritchie in years. Not to mention that Bob had one of his best Saturdays ever. All in all, it turned out to be a good deal for everyone.

Ritchie came back to work Monday and was very pleased with how the bar looked and how fat the till was. His only complaint to Bob was that I checked the till out twice. Bob explained that every Embers manager trainee is trained to check out the till twice a shift. Ritchie's grumbling made it sound like he didn't trust me, but Bob calmed him down and, when I called Ritchie that afternoon, he was full of compliments about how nice the bar looked. "Yeah kid, stop in on your way home from work, I have a envelope with your name on it."

I stopped in and Ritchie slapped the envelope on the bar and he said, "Go ahead, open it."

I shook the envelope and out came $105.00 and I said, "It's more than I expected. I already made $75.00 in tips."

"A deal's a deal, kid, you earned it and I'm glad to pay it."

THE PEE CUSTOMER

Ritchie and I were sitting in the bar about 9:00 one night, talking about the old days. All at once Ritchie says, "Okay kid, I haven't had the lights on in seventeen years, let's turn them on and see how much business we get."

He flipped the lights on and about five minutes later a guy walked in and said, "Where's the can?"

Ritchie stormed out from behind the bar, grabbed the guy, and shoved him out the door exclaiming, "Damn Pee Customer! Shut the lights off kid, all were going to get is Pee Customers."

EMINENT DOMAIN ENDS AN ERA
JUNE 1983

We had all heard the rumors, but couldn't believe that it

was true. The rumor was that developers were going knock down the block that Ritchie's Bar was on and put up a brand new building. Well, when everyone got their notice that they needed to be out by June 15, 1983, it was no longer a rumor.

Ritchie retired and lived permanently at his lake place north of Zimmerman and Bob Peterson's whole crew was out of work for a couple of months until he was able to relocate to the Sexton building a couple of blocks away.

THE END

P.S. Well, it's Monday, May 21, 2007, and I just had breakfast at Peterson's Bacon & Egg Café in Columbia Heights, Minnesota. I had my usual half order of Raspberry Pancakes - still the best in the west. Bob Peterson commented that this was his fourth restaurant and he has never duplicated the one connected to Ritchie's Bar.

Ritchie Koval passed away several years ago, but Bob and I didn't find out until several months later. Yes, Ritchie passed on and the World's Fun Meter backed up a couple notches.

Written: May 21, 2007

BETTY'S TAVERN

COLUMBIA HEIGHTS, MINNESOTA
AUGUST 1974

Yes, I rode past Betty's Tavern every day. And every day I wondered, "What is it like inside?" and "Are the people friendly?"

I took the bus to work at the Sheakley Jensen Adjustment Bureau downtown every day. I just hated riding the bus. As far as I was concerned, riding the bus was stone cold proof that I had screwed up somewhere, somehow. Well, no one on the bus knew me, so what difference did it make. But I knew I'd be embarrassed as could be if one of my former co-workers spotted me getting off the bus.

Every day I rode past Betty's Tavern, I tried to come up with a justification to stop in and have just one cold beer. Then one day, on my way home from work, the bus stopped right in front of Betty's, so I got off and marched right in. My first impression was that I was totally overdressed for this blue-collar bar; in those days, I wore a three-piece suit and carried a brief case. A tall man in his late fifties was the bartender. He approached me and asked, "Are you the insurance man that Mrs. Rossi is waiting to see?"

"No sir, my name is Charlie. I've been waiting all day to have a cold beer."

"Well Charlie, my name is Harold. Harold Ostrum. I'm Mrs. Rossi's head bartender. We sure can fix you up with a cold beer and a couple more after that if that'd be the case."

Just then a man from the end of the bar piped in, "Yah, with twelve stools and three booths, you can see why Betty needs a head bartender."

"Don't mind Harvey, Charlie, he's very free with his comments."

Harvey said, "My name is Harvey Whipps and I just got laid off from

Gambles warehouse where I've worked for thirty-three years. Just what do you Charlie?"

"Well I'm kind of on the comeback trail. I used to be a District Rep for GMAC, but now I do menial office work in downtown Minneapolis."

"In other words, you really didn't come in here to discuss your career potential."

"Okay," Harvey said, "what do you think of those damn Minnesota Twins?"

"I love the Twins. Win or lose, I always love our team."

Then I went on to tell the story about how I cooked the World Series for Embers Restaurants in 1965.

I had my two beers and told Harold and Harvey, "I need to get home to let the dog out. But I'll probably see you to-morrow. I only have about four blocks to go until I get to my house, but I want to beat my wife home from work."

We had a six-year old German Shepherd that stayed inside during the day and needed to be let out as soon as I got home. Luck was with me. I got home with ten minutes to spare, let Schatzie out, and started getting supper together. I was glad to have met Harvey and Harold at Betty's Tavern - it looked like it could be the beginning of an after-work tradition.

HARVEY WHIPPS AND JOANIE

One of the funniest characters at Betty's Tavern was Harvey Whipps. Harvey had worked in Gamble Skogmo's warehouse ever since he got out of the Navy in 1954. He worked the seven a.m. to three p.m. shift and every day, at four p.m., you could count on him sitting on the third stool from the end at Betty's. Harvey was a meticulous reader and after talking to him you really didn't need to read a newspaper or watch TV. Yes, Harvey would give you an unbiased account of the day's events with just a trickle of sarcasm. I can still see Harvey standing at the bar wearing a "Sea Bee" cap and greeting me with, "Well hello Sir Charles, how are the markets doing today?"

Harvey had an on again, off again girlfriend by the name of Joanie. They would sit next to each other at the bar and argue for hours. Harvey's usual response to Joanie's criticism would be, "Go jump in the lake Joanie."

One day I was sitting next to Harvey and he looked over and said to an empty stool, "Go jump in the lake Joanie."

I said, "Harvey, you're talking to an empty stool."

"No problem Sir Charles, just trying to stay in practice."

HAROLD OSTRUM, HEAD BARTENDER & FORMER AUTOMOBILE SALESMAN

Yes, Harold cut quite a suave figure. You would never expect him to be the bartender at Betty's Tavern. Harold was in his late fifties, six foot two and, as he put it, a trim one hundred seventy eight pounds. Harold always wore a burgundy blazer. He wore it so well that even the blue-collar crowd at Betty's didn't give him any grief. Harold liked civilized conversation and if some drunk got too rowdy, he'd tell them, "Your next beer will be served tomorrow."

By the time the drunk figured out what Harold said, he was too embarrassed to order another beer and went home. I said to Harold one time, "You're a pretty classy bartender to be working in a three two bar. How'd you ever end up here?"

"Well Charles, Betty, I mean Mrs. Rossi, needs my help since her husband, Rocky, died. I'm able to help, so I do."

I felt that I'd asked enough questions and let it go at that. What a concept - someone needs help and you can, so you do. Everybody wins.

Harold was a great baseball fan and had played in a semi-pro league when he was in his twenties. One day a friend of mine, Lee Brills, called me and said he had two tickets for the Minnesota Twins and did I want them. Quickly, Harold flashed across my brain and I said, "I'll take them."

When I picked up the tickets, I saw that they were right behind home plate. Boy, was Harold going to be excited! I couldn't wait to get to Betty's that day and tell him the good news.

I walked into the bar that night with a special delivery envelope and delivered the tickets to Harold. As Harold opened up the envelope, a big grin came over his face and he said, "I see that Special Agent Charles has accomplished his secret mission."

Everybody in the bar laughed and was happy for Harold, but I was the happiest. It made me very happy to be able to grant Harold a wish. Harold called me aside and said, "Charles, there's one last concern, and it's that Met Stadium only serves Grain Belt, and I strictly drink Heileman's Old Style."

"Don't worry Harold, you'll be drinking Old Style at the game."

GAME DAY - MINNESOTA TWINS VS. NEW YORK YANKEES

I picked Harold up at Betty's and we drove off to Met Stadium with great anticipation for the game. Harold said, "I could hardly sleep last night knowing that I would see my two favorite teams. It's hard to know who to root for. Who are you rooting for, Charles?"

"I'll root for the Twins because they're the home team. And it was my friend's connection to the Twins that got us these free tickets right behind home plate. And those are two very valid reasons for rooting for the Twins. By the way Harold, you never asked how I would provide the Old Style at the game."

"I don't need to ask Charles, if you say so, I know it will happen."

"Okay Harold, but I've got to tell you. I finally found a use for this three-piece suit. I'll stuff two in my vest and two in my pockets and you'll have four beers for the game."

"But what about you Charles? Are you going to die of thirst?"

"No, I'll buy two vendor beers and save the cups for camouflage."

"A capital plan it is Charles. A capital plan it is."

We arrived at the game and found our seats. They were great seats, right behind home plate. The beer vendor came by and it was time to implement 'Operation Old Style'. I bought two Grain Belts, just to get the cups, then went to the men's room and transferred the Old Style. Harold sat back with his Old Style, reading the roster very softly to me so as not to disturb anyone. The names rolled off his lips, "Harmon Killebrew, Tony Oliva, Rod Carew" and on and on.

I wondered to myself, "Is it more enjoyable to watch

someone else enjoy the game, or watch the game yourself?"

I know I definitely enjoyed watching Harold and I probably would have never gone by myself. The final score was Yankees - three, Twins - two. After the game, we decided to go back to Betty's. On the way there, Harold said, "That certainly was a fine outing. I want to thank you for thinking of me."

"Harold, it was just as much fun for me. We'll do it again when I get some good tickets."

THE NIGHT SHIFT AT BETTY'S

The night shift at Betty's was a completely different group than the day or late afternoon group. Characters materialized at night that I'd only read about. I wondered how they happened to be sitting at Betty's Tavern. Here are a few profiles of the night shift at Betty's.

GEORGE ROCKSTAD & SLIPPERY

George Rockstad was a pipe fitter by trade and used to chum around with his favorite bartender, Slippery. George had served in Korea in the Army's 101st Airborne. As the night progressed, and he got drunker, he'd shout, "Air Borne, Air Borne, all the way."

George worked on the Alaska Pipeline and went out on three-month stints to Alaska. When he returned, he was loaded with money and had a deep thirst.

Slippery was a slightly built man who looked seventy-five, not his true age of thirty-five. I never knew his real name; everybody just called him "Slippery". Slippery was Betty's back up bartender. I once asked Harold, "Why do they call him "Slippery"?"

Harold said, "He just looks slippery and everybody calls him that."

Over a period of four to five years, I never saw Slippery eat. I think he got all his protein from beer.

One night, George and Slippery went barhopping and were pulled over by the Spring Lake Park Police for crossing a white line. Now, George was standing by the squad car reciting a sad story about Korea and the Air Borne and pretty well had the cop convinced to follow him home and not arrest him for a DWI. The cop said, "How about your partner? Is he in any shape to drive?"

"Yes sir. Now, Slippery, is a fine driver. Let me go bring him up here."

George walked back to the car and said, "Now Slippery, you got to shape up and do your best to show the cop you can drive."

Slippery said, "You know me George, I'm ready for anything. Let's go, George."

Slippery stepped out of the car, immediately fell into the ditch, looked up at George and said, "I think I slipped, George."

The cop promptly arrested them both.

Now normally, when people get in trouble, they call home. But not George and Slippery. They called Betty's Tavern. We took up a collection for bail, but it only yielded a hundred bucks and the bail for the two of them was six hundred. Betty asked me what to do. I told her, "Call a bail bondsman. He'll get them released on bond and the bond costs ten percent of bail, or sixty dollars."

I got on the phone and we had the dangerous duo sprung in about an hour - both promising it would never happen again.

THE HENGTSCH SISTERS

Shirley, Dolly, Barb and Debbie, "The Giggler", the infamous Hengtsch sisters, terrorized Betty's Tavern for years. Most of the time they fought amongst each other, but if an outsider made the mistake of interfering, they would all turn on him. The one I remember best was Debbie. She had one continuous giggle. She'd even giggle when she punched her sister.

Harold was the most successful bartender at handling the sisters. He'd negotiate with them and the sisters would settle down for a day. One day, Earl Finch, all one hundred eighteen pounds of him, decided he would butt in. He grabbed Barb Hengtsch by the shoulder and she immediately slammed him against the wall and gave him an elbow to the chin. Earl slid to the floor. On his way down, Barb said, "Mind your own

147

business, Finch."

Most of the time, if the Hengtsch sisters were in the bar, the bar would clear out. Lucky for Betty the sisters finally moved to Wisconsin in 1978.

JACK & AUDREY MORAND

If the term "no account jackass" applied to anyone, it applied to Jack Morand. As luck would have it, he had a very powerful ally in his wife, Audrey. Jack worked at a pallet factory and was always looking for a place to hide so he didn't have to work. One day, his foreman caught him sleeping behind a pile of pallets. The foreman tied a label on his shoe saying, "YOU'RE FIRED JACK". When Jack woke up, he ran to Betty's to cry on Audrey's shoulder. Audrey said, "Don't worry, Jack." And she found him another job in two days.

One time Audrey was sitting by herself when she said to Harold and me, "Do you know why Jack would never leave me boys?" Without waiting for our answer, she continued, "Well, every morning I get up forty-five minutes before Jack and warm his socks and shorts up on the radiator. That way he doesn't have to slide his little butt into cold shorts. Now there you go, what modern woman would do that?"

Harold and I shook our heads. We couldn't think of a single one.

Three years later Audrey came into a large inheritance

and moved Jack to Florida with the promise that he would never have to work again. Harold said, "I can't remember that Jack ever did work, but I hope everything works out for them."

The day before they left, they stopped in at Betty's and bought everyone in the bar a drink. Harvey said, "I wish they were leaving every month."

THE BOWLING MACHINE

Nothing received more attention, or gave more entertainment, than the Bowling Machine. It was a dime per player and up to six could play. Bob Peterson and I used to team up and give the boys a game, but the best duo was Steve Benson, a.k.a. "Zeke, The Streak", and his buddy, Dave. Occasionally a few tourists would stop in at Betty's looking for a easy score, but Zeke and Dave took their money every time and we'd never see the strangers again. If Dave wasn't around, Peterson would sub and the result would be the same.

BETTY SELLS THE TAVERN

By June 1980, Betty was in poor health, so she sold the bar to Roy Choido. Roy was an affable Italian, but his wife was a witch from hell. Roy tried to cover all the shifts himself, but it was wearing him down. I felt sorry for him, so I volunteered to work a couple nights a week even though I was working full-time as a Credit Manager for Minnesota

Truck Center. Working for Roy was great. I'll always remember paydays, because he would slip me a little blue envelope with cash in it and say, "Thanks for your help."

I worked a couple of years for Roy, then went into real estate. I told Roy that I just didn't have time to do everything. Roy was very appreciative and threw me a little party. Even a couple of the Hengtsch sisters stopped in.

EMINENT DOMAIN CLAIMS BETTY'S TAVERN

In 1983 the City of Columbia Heights claimed "Eminent Domain" and the whole block that Betty's Tavern was on was razed and replaced by a small strip mall. Roy was in a state of shock. There he was, sixty-one years old, and the city had taken his livelihood away. Not to mention that the old gang had to find a new place to congregate.

On that fateful day in 1983, when the wrecking ball hit the tavern, Harold and I stood across the street giving a military salute. Now, every time I drive by 42nd and Central, I fondly remember Betty's Tavern and the old gang that used to play there.

THE END

Written: January 16, 2007

Betty's Tavern

CIMAROC CY
The Greatest Salesman of All Time

U.S. ARMY 24TH INFANTRY DIVISION:
AUGSBURG, GERMANY
FEBRUARY 1967

Well, in six months I'd be headed home, Army Discharge
papers in hand, all set to start civilian life. I knew I'd be buying a house because I definitely wanted a hunting dog. I'd
been reading "Field & Stream" religiously and studying the
hunting dog ads in the back. One of the ads read, "Cimaroc
Kennels: pups started and dogs trained: Box 377, Morris,
MN 56087." I wondered to myself, "Where's Morris, Minnesota? And how long of a drive is it from Minneapolis?"

I checked my handy atlas and saw that it was about a one
hundred fifty mile drive from Minneapolis. "Well, that certainly is doable in less than three hours," I thought to myself,
"I think I'll write Cimaroc Kennels and see about the availability of pups when I get out of the Army."

I composed a letter explaining that I'd be getting out
of the Army in August and asking what the availability of
pups would be. Three weeks later, I received a letter with
a picture of a three-month old, black Labrador puppy

retrieving a pigeon wing. Well, as soon as I saw that picture, I was hooked. I felt I wouldn't be satisfied until I had one of those sleek Labradors. I wrote back to Cy Sifers at Cimaroc Kennels asking what the possibility would be of him having a pup when I got out of the service. Cy sent a reply stating that he sold two hundred pups and one hundred trained dogs a year, so there was a strong possibility that he would have a pup ready when I got out of the service. Now my anticipation was red hot. I couldn't wait to get my tour of duty over and get me a pup.

WOLD-CHAMBERLAIN AIRPORT, MINNEAPOLIS, MINNESOTA
AUGUST 31, 1967

I arrived home in Minneapolis, discharged from the Army, with little fanfare, but with a couple of keen thoughts on my mind. The first one was to find housing, so we weren't staying with relatives while we looked for a house to buy. The second was to set up our home so I could have a dog. After a couple of weeks, we found an apartment and, about five months later, we moved into a brand new home in Brooklyn Park with an attached double garage. I built a kennel and attached it to the garage. Then it was time to look for a pup and get the training going.

MORRIS, MINNESOTA
JANUARY 1944

In January 1944, Darrell, 'Cy', Sifers had a very successful restaurant business going called, 'Cy's Coffee Cup'. The restaurant had a steady flow of customers meeting and eating there every day. He also baked cakes for special occasions. But World War II wasn't over and the draft finally caught up with him. A local woman from Morris, Florence Nelson, took over the business and ran it for him while he served in the Army.

In February 1947, Cy Sifers was discharged and arrived home very eager to get his restaurant going again. After going over the books with Florence, Cy was very surprised that he still owed Florence money after she took all the profits. But, no problem, lesson learned. Cy thanked Florence for her service and wrote one last check to her. The restaurant thrived after the war and by 1959 Cy and his wife Mary had six daughters. Sadly, in June of 1960, Mary Sifers died of a heart attack, leaving Cy alone to raise six daughters. He decided to sell the restaurant to give himself more time to take care of his family. He purchased five acres on the edge of Morris and opened up a kennel.

CIMAROC KENNELS IS BORN

Cy pondered what to name the kennel and came up with

the name "Cimaroc". That is, "Ci" for his nick name, "ma" for Mary, his deceased wife, and "roc" for his first field trial Labrador. Cy placed ads in "Field & Stream" and "Sports Afield" magazines advertising pups, started dogs and retriever training. The local town folk laughed at his folly, but no one was laughing when the kennel was filled with dogs for training. Also, pup sales exceeded the number of pups that Cy could produce. Cy had a philosophy that you didn't just breed to produce pups, but the end outcome was to improve the breed. The majority of Cy's business was generated from those little ads in "Field & Stream" and "Sports Afield". Yes, out of those two little ads, at the peak of his sales, Cy was selling two hundred pups and one hundred trained gun dogs. Now, this is one man and one telephone selling a high quality product to a very specific audience.

THE TELEPHONE IS A REMARKABLE SALES TOOL

Yes, the telephone is a remarkable sales tool, but it really depends on who is on the other end. I'll never forget the first time I called to inquire about the possibility of breeding with one of his stud dogs.

"Hello sir, this is Charlie Blanchard in Minneapolis."

The first thing Cy said was, "I remember the name. You wrote me a letter while you were in the Army. I was wondering when you would get around to buying a pup."

"Actually Cy, I have a female whose sire is Field

Champion, "My Rebel", and she just came into season."

"Well Rebel is certainly a fine animal. In fact, he's trained by a friend of mine, Roger Reopelle. The stud fee is two pups or two hundred fifty dollars, but you don't have to make the decision right now. What's the dog's name anyway?"

"Her registered name is, 'Glenwater Glory Be', and she is four years old."

"Well I know the breeding, Chuck. All the Glenwater dogs are from Don Fruen's Kennel. He's the owner of Glenwood Spring Water Company. Just curious, but just how did you happen to get the dog?"

"Well Cy, I was driving past the Humane Society and stopped to see if they had any Labs. Well, low and behold, sitting in this kennel, was a beautiful female, so I went back to the car to get a retrieving dummy. When I showed the dummy to Glory, she immediately fetched it and held, so I could tell she had retriever training. I inquired at the main desk and memorized the phone number of the person who gave her up for adoption. I called and it turned out to be Bernie Mason. He said he went through a divorce and was forced to give her up, but he was glad I got her and sent me the American Kennel Club registration."

"Well Chuck, you're good to go. Bring her out when she's ready. Oh by the way Chuck, how much did you pay for that dog anyway?"

"Twenty dollars, sir."

"My oh my. I could easily sell that dog for $800 and

would pay you $500."

"No Cy, I like the dog, but will keep it in mind for the future."

That phone conversation started a beautiful relationship and I immediately became an unofficial student of Cy Sifer's sales and dog training school.

A couple of weeks later found me making the journey out Highway 55 to Morris, where Glory Be would have a date with Cimaroc Coon Willie. Willie's sire was none other than a young Field Champion, Nassau. Nassau was a real pretty dog and had run the Open at the tender age of 22 months. Cy sung Nassau's praises and, when Nassau reached three years, Cy sold half interest in him to the Lieutenant Governor of Tennessee for $18,500.00. Now, any way you look at it, that's a lot of money in 1965. I asked Cy how he came up with the figure of $18,500.00 and he said, "The customer said 'name your price', so I thought about it and then doubled it."

CIMAROC COON WILLY & GLENWATER GLORY BE HAVE A FINE LITTER OF PUPS

In June 1969, I could not contain my excitement because the pups were due to be born any day. In fact, Glory had not eaten that morning and Cy told me it was a sure sign the pups would be born in the next twenty-four hours. Sure enough, half way through the night, Glory started having pups and I ended up with four females and four males. I gave Cy two pups for the stud fee and sold the remaining six pups locally. It was lot of work, but with the money I realized from the pup sales, I bought my first color TV.

CHARLIE'S DOG JOCKEY SERVICE

One of the things I learned from Cy was how to evaluate older dogs for their resale value. I combed the want ads in the local papers looking for one to four year old Labradors with potential. The beauty of the deal was that I could buy them, generally for one hundred to one hundred fifty bucks, turn around and sell them to Cy for three hundred, Cy would put a little training into them, and get six to seven hundred fifty. This arrangement went on for years and I can't count the times that I headed out to Morris, and then, a couple of months later, I'd receive a nice check. Cy was always realistic and always fair. If I oversold the dog, he let me know and if I missed the obvious, he let me know that too. One time Cy asked me if I thought our arrangement was fair and did it bother me that he made three to four hundred a sale. I said, "Certainly not. You have the investment and are putting your reputation on the line when you sell the dog. Besides, this is how you make your living and I'm just having a little fun learning the dog business."

Later in life, I would find out that Cy was indeed an original and not many people were as honest as him.

About ten years ago I decided to go back in my memory and see if I could come up with how many dogs Cy sold for me and what their names were. After much brain searching I realized that, from 1973 to 1981, I delivered, and Cy sold, about one hundred fifteen dogs with an average of $325.00 paid to me. That comes to a gross sales figure of $37,375.00. No wonder I always had folding money in my pocket at that time.

CIMAROC CY HAS A HEART ATTACK

In June 1981, Cy's second wife, Fern, called from a hotel in Minneapolis to let me know that Cy had had a heart attack and would be having open heart surgery. She was there with her mother, Louise, and daughter, Liza, but was afraid to drive in the city.

"No problem Fern, I'll be down there with my Stutz Bear Cat to pick you all up and drive you to the hospital."

The problem was I didn't have a Stutz Bear Cat. I had a Renault LeCar, which was a very small car. Luckily, with a lot of squeezing, I was able to fit Fern, her mother and little Liza, who was only ten years old at the time, into the car. The operation went as well as any triple by-pass can go, but Cy never seemed the same again. I could see in his eyes that life in general just wasn't that much fun anymore. I drove Fern and her family to the hospital every day to see him, but when Fern and I were alone she asked me, "Is he depressed?"

"Well Fern, he's had major surgery and I would say, give it some time and things should look better."

During the next couple of years I could see that running the kennel was a struggle for Cy and he started looking for a buyer for the business. I considered it, but no way did I want to live way out in Morris, Minnesota.

CY SELLS CIMAROC KENNELS

June 1983 was a bittersweet time for my old friend. He found a local, qualified buyer for the business, but also ended up getting divorced from Fern. Cy's health still wasn't that great and how his marriage ended up in divorce he never told me. It was hard to see an old friend go through tough times and not know what to do to help. I certainly wasn't taking sides, Fern was a friend of mine too, so I remained neutral on the matter.

I met the new owner of Cimaroc Kennels and felt an instant distrust for the guy and will not mention his name in this story. All I can say, whatever you do in life, always trust your instincts. I put a couple dogs on consignment with the new owner, but ended up never getting paid. I was naive enough to take the matter to Stevens County Conciliation Court, but the judge ruled against me saying I couldn't prove I didn't get the dogs back.

I related the story to a friend of mine and he said, "You never will receive justice in a small town."

That information didn't make me feel any better, but it will certainly guide me in the future.

CIMAROC CY RETIRES TO MEXICO

In 1985, Cy thought about retiring to his home state of Missouri and selling a few dogs, but his banker convinced him it was cheaper to retire in Mexico. So Cy decided to packed up and live in Mexico from September to April.

It wasn't the best connection, but I could reach Cy by phone down in Mexico. He didn't want to talk long and spend my money so freely, but I could tell he was lonely. He said the weather was a very consistent 85 degrees with a 5 mph wind blowing in from the ocean. He said he had a very nice apartment right on the beach and the rent was only three hundred and fifty per month. There were a few other Americans, but mostly he was there by himself trying to learn Spanish so he could converse with the locals. All those years of talking to everybody across the country, and now he was living in a place where he didn't speak the language. It must've been really rough. Cy spent two more winters in Mexico, but even the winters in Minnesota seemed okay compared to the isolation of Mexico.

MORRIS, MINNESOTA

In 1989, I drove out to Morris to buy a trained hunting dog from the new owner of Cimaroc Kennels and spent the rest of the day with Cy. We recalled old times and I thanked him for all the lessons he had taught me about dogs and about life. We promised to get together again soon, but I had a very strong feeling that this was the last time I would ever see him. Cy said his health had been failing and that he was going to go to Oklahoma to live with his daughter. I said, "You have my address and phone, drop me a line or call me with the new information."

I never did hear from Cy again, but I heard rumors that he had suffered a stroke and was unable to speak.

ROSEVILLE, MINNESOTA

In 1999, I moved into a new property in Roseville, Minnesota and, when I stopped into the local coffee shop, I ran into Zeke "The Streak" Benson. Zeke had grown up in Morris, Minnesota and purchased pups from Cy. I told Zeke of my many attempts to locate Cy, but he told me, "Sorry, but your friend died of a stroke in Oklahoma in 1998. And that guy could sell ice to an Eskimo and the Eskimo would love it."

"Here, here." We hoisted our glasses, "To Cimaroc Cy, the greatest salesman of all time."

THE END

Written: April 3, 2007

HEIDI THE WIREHAIR
& THE STATE OF HUNTING
A Fifty Year History of Pheasant Hunting

PAPER ROUTE: COLBY, WISCONSIN
NOVEMBER 1957

I was making the usual rounds of my paper route when I was stopped by George Sterzinger to discuss just about every subject under the sun, but especially the state of hunting. "Well Chucky," said George, "did you get a pheasant this year with your dog, Schooner?"

"Yes sir, we got two so far: one when I went out with Tommy Hoffman and my dog Schooner and one last week down by Grampa VanSlett."

"Well, you better enjoy it now because, by the time you reach my age, you'll be paying to hunt or hunting will be banned all together."

Now George offered that opinion even though he never went hunting a day in his life and considered the activity foolhardy and wasteful. It was often said that the Sterzingers were so tight that they would pinch a nickel until the buffalo said uncle.

I said, "Well George, no matter what happens, I will

always be a pheasant hunter and will always have a good dog."

"Well Chucky, I hope you can keep that promise to yourself. But what if a woman comes along and tells you different."

"What woman would that be George?"

"Well, it could be the woman you marry - you know women run the roost, that's why I never got married."

"Well George, that's all well and good, but I'm only twelve years old and I don't think I'll be marrying any time soon."

"You say that now, but some day you'll be forced into a choice and the poor dog will be left in the cold."

"No George, if that situation ever arises, I will pick the dog."

PHEASANT HUNTING IN THE 1950s

Before I was old enough to drive a car, I'd put Schooner, my English Springer Spaniel, on a lead and we'd walk to the woods. Yes, at thirteen years old I would put my twelve-gauge pump in a case, sling it over my shoulder, and walk down the railroad tracks to my Grampa and Gramma VanSleet's to occasionally roust up a pheasant. And by occasionally, I mean maybe three birds a season. But, if I was lucky enough to score, Gramma VanSleet would gladly cook up the bird for me and complete the feast with mashed potatoes and gravy. Gramma would say, "You and Schooner must know what you're doing."

Grampa would say, "You got a pheasant, you should get your picture in the paper. I haven't seen a pheasant in thirty years."

Now, if I asked my mother to cook up my pheasant she'd say, "No, I'm not cooking that nasty thing."

George Sterzinger's words were ringing in my mind. Maybe some day I would marry a woman like my mother and be out of luck for someone to cook what I got. But, as time went on, I learned to cook for myself and I never had to ask anybody again - I just went ahead and cooked the meal myself.

PHEASANT HUNTING IN THE 1960'S

Most of the 1960s were taken up by my service in the Army, a stint at school, and a marriage. It's hard to explain the cultural differences between someone who grew up in a small town and someone who grew up in a city, but when I told my wife, Andrea, that I was leaving at 5:30 a.m. to go pheasant hunting, she looked at me like I was crazy. She let me pursue my hobby, however, and the first dog I started hunting with in the late sixties was a Labrador named, "Glen Water Glory Be". Glory Be was a four-year old female that had been professionally trained, but given up for adoption to the Humane Society. The reason the previous owner gave

167

was that he was going through a divorce and his wife threw him and his dogs out. I passed by the Humane Society and noticed Glory Be in the kennel and could tell she was a well-bred dog. I bought her on the spot for the princely sum of twenty dollars. We hunted together for a couple years before I sold her to a fellow in Michigan for seven hundred dollars. Glory Be was an adequate pheasant dog but her real talent was as a duck dog.

The pheasant hunting in Minnesota was spotty - you could drive all day and the dog might pick up one rooster. This certainly wasn't the kind of hunting I had heard about when I grew up in Wisconsin and it made me feel sorry for the dog. Here the dog trains all year to hunt a few weekends in the fall and this was all the action we could give them. Yes, the 1960s ended up with me being introduced to some good dog work, but overall, not much pheasant action.

PHEASANT IN THE 1970'S

Now, if the pheasant hunting was spotty in the 1960s, in was just plain abundant the 1970s. I raised two Labrador pups up who turned out to be great pheasant dogs. The first pup was a male named Cimaroc CC Rider. Now, CC was a perfect physical specimen of what a Labrador should look like and the most trainable dog I ever owned. If someone had downed a bird and had no idea where it was, you could just say to CC, "Dead bird down. Hunt 'em up." It wasn't but a matter of minutes before CC was back with the bird in his mouth, sitting next to you holding the bird, and wagging his tail. During this time, I discovered hunting in South Dakota. A group of us: myself, Harlan Anderson, a car dealer from Jackson, Minnesota, and two of his salesman, went on a trip to Howard, South Dakota. I pulled a four-compartment dog trailer and had CC Rider, Mr. Thrifty, a large male Labrador, Jimmy Beam, a male Golden Retriever, and Lads Pride & Joy Heidi, a female Labrador. We ran two dogs at a time and, even with four dogs, it was hard to keep up with all the action. By the end of the weekend, we had our limit of twenty-four birds, the dogs were tired, and we were tired. I was never in favor of hunting in groups, but this foursome worked out pretty good.

HUNTING PARTNERS - PETE RUCKVINA

Now, the best hunting partner I've ever had was a fellow named Pete Ruckavina. How we met is an unusual story and how we lost track of each other is another story. In the early 1970s, I used to have coffee with Pete's mother, Gloria, and she mentioned that her son, who was my age, was an avid hunter. Pete and I met and I sold him a Labrador pup named Digger, who turned out to be an outstanding hunting dog. Pete was living in Minneapolis when I met him, but he was a plumber by trade and the City of Fairmont, Minnesota paid to move him to Fairmont to be the town plumber.

Well, as luck would have it, Fairmont sits smack dab on the border of Minnesota and Iowa. It was just about this time that pheasant populations really picked up in Iowa, so Pete would scout the territory and find the best hunting spots. One weekend I went down with Goldie, a Yellow Labrador sired by the National Field Champion, Del Tone Buck. Goldie was a seasoned veteran and I had campaigned her in field trials where she brought home the trophy more than once. Pete and I set out in the morning to hunt ducks and pheasant with Goldie and Digger. First, we hit the sloughs, walking through them with waders, and filled our limit of mallards in about two hours. With that done, we were ready to move on to pheasant hunting. Now Goldie wasn't a great pheasant dog, but she was probably the best water dog I had ever hunted with. But Pete's Digger was a great pheasant dog and on that day, we had our limit of six pheasants in about two hours. Well, with that kind of efficiency, by noon, we had our limits of both pheasants and ducks and were in time to watch the kickoff of the Vikings.

This hunting partnership went along for a number of years until Pete and his wife, Nancy, found religion. I should have known something was up when I saw the PTL sticker on his bumper. Praise the Lord Foundation was an organization founded by Jim and Tammy Faye Baker. It was deemed a fraudulent organization some years later, disbanded, and Jim Baker went to prison. When I called Pete about hunting, he was very vague, so then I talked with our mutual friend Cy

Sifers, a professional dog trainer. Cy said that Pete had gone completely nuts: he sold his dog and his gun and had given his life to the Lord. I decided to drive down to Fairmont to talk with Pete in person, but when I arrived, his house was empty and none of the neighbors knew where he moved. Now, that was twenty-three years ago and I have tried, on and off, to locate Pete, but with no success. I've hunted in small groups and I've hunted in large groups, but no better times did I have than when I had Pete Ruckavina for a hunting partner.

PHEASANT HUNTING IN THE 1980s

Hunting was great in the first half of the 1980s, but nonexistent the second half because of personal problems and divorce. But this is a story about hunting, so let me continue on with hunting, dogs, and people I encountered.

I used to hunt, on and off, with Tom Leehane and Woody Woodall. We would gas up my old Ford wagon and head down Rochester, Minnesota way. The hunting was pretty good and the three of us would generally come away with three birds or so. We used my yellow female, Goldie, and an up and coming puppy named Riders Andy. Now, Andy was a big, long-legged Labrador and weighed ninety-seven pounds even after training three times a week. I have never owned a retriever with a better nose or a nicer dog to have around than Andy.

ANDY AND THE VOLKSWAGEN

I bought a Volkswagen Beetle with a sunroof and spent many happy Sunday afternoons driving with Andy in the passenger seat, searching for pheasants on the back roads around Rochester. Andy would lean out the window and, as soon as he saw a bird, he'd start wagging his tail. I'd pull over and the race was on. Andy would catch up to the bird and I would get ready to shoot. This partnership worked great, so I decided to enter Andy in a couple of field trials. The spectators were impressed by his performance, so much so that, one of them, the head trainer for Olin kennels in St. Louis, made me an offer of five thousand dollars for Andy. Much as I could have used the money, the dog was just too special, so I turned him down. One year later, at the age of three and a half, Andy died of cancer. That was one of the saddest days of my life, but I choose to remember the days when Andy was big and strong and we were tooling down the back roads of Rice County looking for roosters.

LUKE, THE GERMAN SHORT HAIR

Most of my life I had been brainwashed to believe that the Labrador is the only dog to have as a hunting companion. Well, that belief was completely dismantled after I purchased a two-year old male German Short Hair named Luke. First of all, hunting pheasants with a pointer versus hunting with a flushing dog is like night and day. The pointer holds the bird so you know right where it is, whereas the flushing dog or the retriever trails the pheasant until the bird flushes; two completely different hunting styles. For my money, too see a Pointer quarter into the wind and then lock up on point is heaven on Earth.

Luke was a good Pointer and so much more; it was hard to believe he was real. Luke could learn just about any trick you wanted to teach him and seemed to understand just exactly what I said. For instance, one night I was sitting in a motel after a hard days hunt in South Dakota, watching a Western on TV. I got on the floor and told Luke, "Let's crawl and sneak up on the Indians." Sure enough, Luke crawled right with me and when I said, "Put your head down", Luke put his muzzle on the floor and looked over at me, his tail wagging. I had to give Luke away in 1985 because of personal problems, but we had some interesting adventures while we were together; in fact, in a later story, I will go into more detail.

PHEASANT HUNTING IN THE 1990s

In 1993, an old friend of mine, Don Balsimo, invited me along to South Dakota to go hunting. I had been without a dog since giving Luke away in1985, but Don's son, Todd, had two Brittany Spaniels named Smoke and Red. A total of six of us went out, but the birds were slim and we came

home with just two apiece. The pheasant population continued to decline for the next couple of years so we decided not
to go out again until 1996. By that time, Red had run away,
never to be seen again, and Todd had sold Smoke, so I invited a young friend of mine, Joel Manns, along because Joel
had two German Wirehair Pointers. I'd never hunted behind
a Wirehair before and was curious to see what they could do.
Well, Joel trotted out Casey, a large, older male, and Mag-
gie, a young female. Boy, did we get a show. I have never
hunted behind a better combination and it wasn't long before
we filled our limit for the day. After that, I was completely
sold on Wirehairs.

THINGS ARE HAPPENING, APRIL 1999

Well, come June 10, 1999, big things are happening. Big,
big things: I'm getting married to Joan Breen, we're buying
a house in Roseville, and space has been set aside for my
future hunting companion's kennel. Joel Manns called me
up to tell me about a six-year old female German Wirehair
being advertised on the Internet, "I think you should check
it out."

It ended up that the person who owned the Wirehair was
a seventeen-year old rich kid by the name of Jeffery Dumont
who lived down in the Southwestern corner of Minnesota.
Jeffery was just long on dogs. He had three other pointers
and was looking to move this female Wirehair named Heidi.

He sent a picture and told me he had hunted her since she was eight-months old. I was really interested in the dog, but told him that I couldn't take her until September, when we were in the new house. Jeffery and I made our deal, with Jeffery agreeing to keep Heidi until I could pick her up in September.

HEIDI THE WIREHAIR

Things with the new house got delayed, so I was finally able to pick up Heidi on the opening of pheasant season in October 1999. I drove down to Cyrus, Minnesota, which was a three and a half hour drive, and met Jeffrey Dumont at 8:30 a.m. Jeffrey loaded up Heidi, who looked just like her picture, and we headed out to pheasant country. Well, it didn't take long for Heidi to show me she was the real deal - in an hour's time, she pointed five roosters and two hens. We ended up with four fine roosters and I thought, "Jeffrey is crazy to let this dog go." I told him, "Everything looks fine" and handed him a check.

SETTLING IN

I drove home Saturday night, installed Heidi in her new kennel, and heard not a peep all night. I got up at 4:30 Sunday morning only to find that she had gotten out. I got on the phone with a kennel distributor and picked up more panels to make a top to prevent Heidi from jumping out.

Yes, this six-year old dog could still clear a six-foot fence, but once I secured the extra panels, Heidi the escape artist was contained. The next problem was that she would take off for long runs. About once a week, she would somehow get away from me, but after two years of chasing her, she finally settled down. Am I sorry I bought her? Certainly not, she is the finest canine athlete I have ever owned.

HUNTING ACCOMODATIONS

I have stayed in more old hotels and motels than I care to remember. One particularly fond memory is of the Calico Hotel in Union City, South Dakota. Laurie Olson, the proprietor, cooked wonderful breakfasts and even packed us a lunch. Even if I was with a big group of guys, I made sure that I had a room of my own. One night I had an unexpected visitor. Another hunter tied his German Short Hair, Gretchen, to my door and every time I got up to go to the bathroom, Gretchen ended up in my room. I finally let her in the room and she slept at the end of the bed. Her master called for her in the morning, but she just lay there, wagging her tail. I got up and told her master that it was easier to let her sleep in the room than to navigate around her and the door. Everybody had a good chuckle and Gretchen just sat there, wagging her tail. And Gretchen kind of reminded me of my old dog Luke, so it was kind of fun to have the company.

IF THE HUNTING IS SLOW EAT PIE

If the hunting was slow, I always managed to find a restaurant that had good pies. One of the best was a little place in Dolliver, Iowa called Grandma B's. Grandma B (I never learned her real name) served up Banana Cream, Lemon Meringue, and the best Dutch Apple you ever tasted. I stopped in so many times, she thought I lived in the area.

PHEASANT HUNTING 2006

In 2006, Heidi, at thirteen, still had the desire to hunt, but I had to take it real easy with her. During the year, we were at the Apple River Hunt Club twice and she had six solid points. Although she didn't see well enough to retrieve anymore, her nose is as good as ever.

HAPPY COUPLE FROM DIFFERENT BACKGROUINDS

Joan and I have been married seven wonderful years and, to my delight, she loves my pheasant recipe. It is as follows:

ROAST PHEASANT

One quartered Pheasant. Dip in Flour, Egg, and Seasoned Bread Crumbs. Brown and set aside in Baking Dish.

Combine the following ingredients:

1 can Cream of Mushroom Soup

½ cup onion diced

1 four-ounce can of cut up mushrooms

1 cup Apple Juice

1 clove Garlic

1 teaspoon Worchester Sauce

Salt & Pepper to taste

Pour this combination over the bird and bake at 350 degrees for one and one half hours.

Give this a try - I know you will love it.

THE END

P.S. George Sterzinger was right - in 2006, we are paying to hunt.

Written: October 18, 2006

THE BRACELET

So, here I am at the Hidden Harbor Lounge at the Shorewood Inn in Fridley, Minnesota. At yet another informal business meeting. What a joke, "business meeting" - the only person doing business is the owner, Jimmy Nikklow. He owns the business and the rest of us are just there. What we're hanging on for is hope. We are hoping that we'll make that one contact that will catapult our careers from so-so to the big time. I watch Jimmy Nikklow as he walks around the restaurant and bar checking on the things that need to be checked on. He's dressed impeccably in a two thousand dollar suit. He is also wearing a gold bracelet that must be worth at least two thousand dollars. I thought to myself, "Now that's what I need, a fancy bracelet. Because wearing that bracelet will show the world that I have arrived."

Yes, this is the imaginary world that one inhabits when all your spare time is spent in bars. I was fixated on attaining success, but it had to be success defined in a monetary way. And it wasn't important that just I knew, the whole world had to know. So how was I going to scrape together two thousand dollars to buy that bracelet? Now, my mother's voice was in my head saying, "Do a good job and the money will follow. Quit worrying about how much money you're making."

If only I could just trust that it was all going to work out. But right then, I was fixated on that gold bracelet - and I wouldn't be satisfied until I had one.

BIG MIKE AND BILLY THE GOLD MAN

Mike Kelly and Billy Meyers were part of the gang of cronies that I hung out with at the Shorewood. Mike was a manufacturer's rep for the machine industry and he cut quite an intimidating figure standing six foot six and weighing about two hundred eighty pounds. But looks can be deceiving. Mike had a heart of gold and was gentle as a lamb. He loved to sit in the bar, drink beer, and talk shop all night long. The reason he ran around with Billy Myers, also known as, 'Billy, the Gold Man', was that Billy was a pretty good listener and he actually seemed interested in what Mike had to say. Billy and Mike sat at the end of the bar and talked for hours about the stock market, gold prices, and whatever else caught their interest. Fifty beautiful women could walk by and they would never even look up.

Now, Billy the Gold Man was a survivor. Not just in the physical sense, but also in the psychological sense. He'd been in the Army during the Viet Nam War and had been shot in the head and left for dead. Eventually, somebody in his unit found him and he was sent him back to the States where he recuperated for six months in a Veterans Hospital. Amazingly, you could hardly see the scar on the side of his head, but he did have monster headaches all day long. Billy never complained or raised his voice but just sat quietly listening to Mike's stories.

Billy had a hefty pension from the Army, but made additional income buying gold from dentists' offices and reselling it to jewelry stores. How doing this operation with the dentists made any money I was never privy to, but Billy seemed to be at it every day - meeting with dentists and making a deal for the gold. I suggested that he work on the dental labs rather than individual dentists and even volunteer to vacuum the carpets for gold chips and pieces. Billy said he'd look into it, but he never told me if he did or not.

EXTRA! EXTRA! READ ALL ABOUT IT!
BILLY & MIKE ARE GOING TO BE RICH!

Yes, that was the word going around the Shorewood. Mike had made a deal on some plastic manufacturing equipment and they were going to be equipment brokers. The machine was a steal at twenty-seven thousand dollars, but would have to be stored until it was sold. Mike had approached the Industrial Development Department in Hibbing, Minnesota and found that he could possibly sell the machine to them for eighty thousand dollars. Mike was boasting that they'd make a cool profit of fifty-three thousand dollars when Russ Goldman, the liquor salesman, pointed out that it would be a hefty freight bill from Kansas City, Missouri to Minneapolis and then on to Hibbing. Mike said, "Don't worry about that. We'll cover all the angles and make sure we come out on top. Billy won't have to peddle gold anymore and we can just manage our machine brokerage and not have to travel so much."

In the next couple of weeks, Mike and Billy rented some industrial space and waited for delivery of their fancy machine. The expenses of start up and moving the machine exhausted all the spare cash that either of them had. But if they could just hold out until the sale was complete, they would be in fat city. The weeks dragged on and on and there were countless meetings with the Industrial Development Committee. Eventually, the funding collapsed and no sale was likely happen in the near future. The strain was evident on Billy and Mike's faces as the months passed by. Yes, the expenses of rent, utilities, et cetera were draining all their extra cash and no sale was forthcoming. Finally, after months of frustration, they sold the machine, at a loss, to a small company and ended any further interest in the used machinery business.

JUDGEMENTS WEIGH HEAVILY ON NEW HOME BUYERS

Billy the Gold Man was picking up the pieces of his business fiasco with Mike and ended up with sixty-eight thousand dollars in judgments against him. The big problem was that his wife had secured a really good job in northern Minnesota and they were trying to buy a new home. As soon as the mortgage company saw all those judgments, they said they would have to be satisfied before the company would close on the property. Mike thought and thought, but no way could he come up with the money.

CHARLIE THE CREDIT MAN TO THE RESCUE

Billy was relating his credit problems to Mike one night and seemed overwhelmed about how to resolve it. Mike said, "Charlie has more than twenty years of credit experience, maybe he can work on getting the judgments settled for you."

I said, "I'll sure try. Once your creditors find out that you're judgment proof they should be more than willing to accommodate our request."

Billy replied, "What do you mean 'judgment proof'?"

"Well Billy, it's like this. You receive an Army pension and that pension is completely exempt from garnishment or levy of any kind. The net effect for the creditor is that, judgment or not, there is no way they can touch your money. So my suggestion is this - gather all your bills and the name of the collection agency that has them and send them to me. Once I receive them, and put them in a nice pile, I will work on settling them for forty percent, or forty cents on the dollar. That means that the sixty-eight thousand dollars in judgments will clear out and settle in full for twenty-seven thousand two hundred dollars. That works out to be a savings of forty thousand eight hundred dollars for you and you'll be able to go ahead and buy your house. So gather up all your bills tonight and I'll meet with you tomorrow and to discuss Operation 'Make Them Go Away'."

"That's sounds great Charlie, but what is this going to cost me?"

"This will not cost you any cash at all. What I have in mind should be pretty easy for the 'Gold Man' to obtain. If I settle these old judgments for forty cents on the dollar, I want a gold bracelet just as nice as Jimmy Nikklow's."

Billy said, "You're on. I'll have the list of judgments dropped off at your place by my son tomorrow. Once this is over Charlie, I'll give you the address of the jeweler and he will place the bracelet on your wrist."

NEGOTIATING WITH CREDITORS & COLLECTION AGENCIES

I started the process of negotiating settlements with Billy

the Gold Man's eight creditors. I soon discovered that most of the files were all with collection agencies and they would not talk to me unless Billy faxed a letter saying I was his representative. We put a form letter together and I started making my contacts.

I immediately met resistance. On the first call the collection manager didn't believe that anyone was judgment proof. I was calm and deliberate and explained that our offer was not negotiable and that I would check back in two weeks.

TWO WEEKS LATER

Finally, I called one of the creditors and they accepted the offer, but put a contingency on it. The contingency was that the certified funds had to be received within thirty days. I requested that they fax a letter to me showing the terms of the settlement and then moved on to the next creditor. The next creditor balked a little bit, but I explained that I had reached a settlement with the first creditor and that the offer was only good if all creditors settled in thirty days. In other words, Billy would not get the house unless all his judgments were settled and there was no sense paying the money to settle one if we couldn't settle them all.

THREE WEEKS LATER

Now, as I made my follow up calls to the creditors, things were beginning to fall into place. Apparently they had had time to analyze the situation and I was pushing the deadline pretty hard. I explained that if things went according to plan, I would deliver a cashier's check for the settlement amount in exchange for a satisfaction of judgment.

Mr. Murphy, one of the collection agency managers, recognized my name and said that I interviewed with him. I acknowledged the interview and he replied, "Yes, you're the guy that sent me that letter."

I said, "What letter?"

"The letter that said that 'if you pay peanuts, you get monkeys, so you must have a bunch of monkeys working there.'"

I said, "I apologize for the letter, but I am perfectly serious about this matter and guarantee you that, if you have the satisfaction of judgment ready, I will personally deliver the cashier's check to you. If you're still mad about the letter, you can chew me out when I get there."

"No, I'm not mad Charlie, but I did think that we would have made a pretty good team and was very disappointed. And one of the employees found the letter and all day they were singing "We're The Monkeys". But, I got it off my chest now and feel a lot better now that I talked to you. Let's work together and make this settlement happen."

I said, "Amen. I will see you with the check soon."

SETTLEMENT DAY

I met Billy the Gold Man early on Monday morning. He

had eight cashier's checks totaling twenty-seven thousand two hundred dollars and it was time to make the deliveries. After I delivered the checks and picked up the satisfactions of judgment, Billy could go to work and clear up his credit bureau. I had taken a vacation day from my regular job to get it done and met Billy at four p.m. at the Shorewood with the satisfactions in hand. "Well Charlie, this is great. When do you want to pick up your bracelet?"

"Well Billy, let's do that next month. That will give you time to work on your credit bureau and me longer to anticipate getting the bracelet."

"Okay Charlie. Next month I'll call you and give you the address of the jeweler who has your bracelet. All you have to do is show your ID and the jeweler will strap it on your wrist."

THIRTY DAYS LATER

Billy called me at five thirty a.m. and said, "Daylight in the swamp Charlie. Your bracelet is waiting for you at a jewelry shop in St. Louis Park."

He gave me the directions and phone number and I called the jeweler to tell him I'd be stopping by at six p.m. I arrived at the shop and the jeweler got the bracelet and laid it on a piece of black velvet. It was just beautiful, but I could sense a little hesitation on the jeweler's part. Finally, he spoke up and said, "Listen. Billy gave me a check for this bracelet and

I've had problems with Billy's checks before. Would you mind waiting twenty-four hours until the check clears?"

"Well sir, nobody understands your situation more than I do. I will call tomorrow and then come and pick up the bracelet."

TWENTY-FOUR HOURS LATER

I called the jeweler and, as anticipated by me, the check has cleared and everything was good to go. I drove out and the jeweler was all smiles as he installed the bracelet on my wrist. "Charlie, you knew yesterday that the check would clear and never had a doubt did you?"

"No sir. I consider myself a student of human moves and I have no doubts with Billy."

I didn't make any fuss because I know sometimes things can take extra time. With that, I bid my farewell and drove home sneaking glimpses at the bracelet, feeling very pleased and saying to myself, "Well tomorrow, right after work, I'll dress up in a suit and head over to the Shorewood and show the boys my new acquisition."

THE UNVEILIING

I was curious as to the value of the bracelet, so I took it to my friend, Nick. Nick was the jeweler who worked next door to Peterson's Coffee Shop. Nick checked it out and said it was 14-carat gold and weighed 23-penny weight with an estimated retail value of eighteen hundred to two thousand dollars. I told Nick the whole story and he laughed and said, "You certainly have your ways."

Later that night at the Shorewood, I was anticipating the boys' reaction, but the only guy in the bar was a retired car salesman. Yes it was old Ben who I knew from my days at GMAC. Ben was a non-stop talker, always talking about himself. Ben noticed the bracelet and said, "That's not real gold is it?"

"It certainly is. I just had it appraised by Nick and it's 14-carat gold for your information."

Jimmy Nikklow stopped by and said, "Nice bracelet. Very nice bracelet, Charlie." But deep down, I couldn't shake Ben's reaction. I drank up and on the way home questioned whether I would ever wear it again. You know, you see those guys wearing fake Rolexes and jewelry, and I certainly didn't want to be thought of as part of that group.

SARAH KINNEY'S CHRISTMAS PARTY
DECEMBER 2006

Well, here it is, about eighteen years later and the only time I wear the bracelet is when I attend Sarah's annual Christmas Party. Sarah is my wife Joan's best friend and a very successful realtor. Every year Sarah throws a fabulous party for her clients and friends and it's a really good excuse to get all dressed up.

I have come many miles from the person that I was when I thought that monetary wealth was the fast lane to happiness. I have not been in a bar, nor have I taken a drink, in years and now I am in search of spiritual growth. The bracelet lies in my jewelry box and my wife Joan says, "If it doesn't mean anything, give it away."

"Oh, but it does mean something. It reminds me of what's not important."

THE END

Written: April 06, 2007

The Bracelet

OUT OF THE DARK
AND INTO THE LIGHT

ANIMAL HUMANE SOCIETY: ST. PAUL,MN
NOVEMBER 30, 2006

It's 11:45 a.m. and I'm waiting for the Animal Humane Society to open up at noon. I'm here because Heidi the Wirehair died last night and I've come to drop off her body. This is about as sad a sight as can be: an old man sitting in a van with the body of his old hunting dog who died at the age of thirteen and one half years. I had taken Heidi to the vet just three days ago and they said she had a very bad heart murmur. The vet suggested doing tests to see exactly what was wrong, but my reply was, "I have been down this road too many times before, Doctor. You run six hundred dollars worth of tests and the dog dies on the table. I think I'll take her home and make her comfortable." I could see by the vet's eyes that it wouldn't be long.

So here I am, feeling sad and waiting for the Humane Society to open up. Finally, I see somebody moving inside and can't take it anymore – I'm going in to see what's happening. I walk around to the back door and meet a young woman who said, "Can I help you?"

"My dog died yesterday," I said, my voice breaking, "and I need to drop the body off."

I started thinking that my mother died in July and I didn't have this much emotion. Maybe this was a combination of both losses weighing down on me and I couldn't keep it in any longer. The young woman said, "My name is Sarah and I am very sorry for your loss, but you have to wait in your car or the waiting room."

I went back to my van and about twenty minutes later they opened up. Two brothers were ahead of me and I overheard that they were giving up their father's cat because their father had passed away the day before and nobody wanted the cat. This made me think that a person needs to plan ahead to make sure the family is taken care of but also the pets. I was calmly waiting until it was my turn when a volunteer came in to pick up a yellow Labrador that she was going to keep for a couple of weeks. I volunteered to hold the dog while she secured a traveling crate and dog food. The Lab's name was Rachel and she was one sleek machine. A little too much energy for the average Joe, but just holding her and having her sit brought back memories to this old dog man. Finally, it was my turn and the young lady who took the information was a perfect example of sincerity and kindness. I told her, "Heidi is wrapped in a blanket in back of the van and I really don't want to see her go."

I gave my keys to the attendant and she went outside and brought Heidi in through the back door, out of my line of sight. So that's it. Now I'm all alone with my memories after seven and a half years of daily walks and numerous hunting trips. I called my wife, Joanie, to give her the news and drove back to work. Yes, this will be a big adjustment and I sure hope it's busy at work.

SIX HOURS LATER

Well, I'm home from work and would normally be feeding Heidi, but, going to her kennel, all I see is the porcelain dog dish that Joanie made for me in clay class. It's a beautiful creation from my wonderful artist and is one of my prized gifts. The interior reads "Good Boy" and the outside reads "Charlie's Pal" because originally we thought I would get a male dog. "What to do? What to do? I can't mope around in a daze," I thought to myself. Then I remembered my Grandma VanSleet's words, "Chucky, it's not what happens to a person, it's what you do about it." That's the answer. It's sad that Heidi died, but she lived thirteen and a half years and had a great life. What I needed to do was to get another dog.

THE HUNT FOR THE HUNTER

Now, I had to face facts: I'd be sixty-two in April and simply didn't have time to wait for a pup to grow up. Also, one of my core beliefs had always been that a dog doesn't belong in the house, especially a hunting dog. That settled, I grabbed the paper and spotted these two ads:

GERMAN SHORT HAIR MALE 4 YRS OLD
GOOD HUNTER MUST SELL $250.00
PHONE: 320-XXX-XXX

I called and spoke to Wayne who said that "Clyde" was a good hunter, but he had to sell him because he needed to take over the complete operation of the family farm due to his father's poor health. "I just don't have time and it's not fair to the dog."

I told Wayne that I'd be out to look at Clyde on Saturday, but would call Friday to confirm.

GERMAN SHORT HAIR FEMALE 16 MONTHS
STARTED HUNTER NEEDS GOOD HOME $250.00
PHONE: 651-XXX-XXXX

I called and spoke to Ron who said that "Bella" was a nice dog that he had raised out of his last litter. The dog actually belonged to his daughter, but she was going through a divorce and couldn't keep the dog any longer. I noticed that Ron lived in Scandia, Minnesota, which was close to my friend Joel Manns' place, so I arranged for Joel to head over and check out the dog for me. That was fine with Ron and Joel said he'd stop by on Thursday night to check out Bella.

Two good possibilities here and I looked forward to seeing what would happen.

THURSDAY NIGHT: "BELLA REPORT"
NOVEMBER 30, 2006

Joel Manns and I had hunted together, on and off, for over five years. Joel's father, Charlie Manns, and I had been friends for over fifteen years. No one I know in this world has more integrity than Joel Manns, so whatever he told me about Bella, I would believe. Unfortunately for Bella and me, it wasn't a very good report. Joel said he stopped by and Bella seemed "birdy": she was very friendly, but small - she didn't weigh thirty pounds. Now, I don't like scrawny dogs and, even though I wanted to get a dog, I knew this wouldn't work out. On Friday morning, I called Ron and thanked him for taking the time to show the dog to Joel, but I would have to pass.

I gave a quick call to Wayne about the four-year old male German Short Hair and Wayne said he had just sold the dog. "Yes Sir," Wayne said, "a large proportioned woman bought him and I know he will be well fed. Sorry you missed him, but thanks for calling back."

Darn. Two possibilities and both fizzled out.

FRIDAY NIGHT: DECEMBER 1, 2006

I picked up a paper and was looking through the ads when I spotted an ad for Chocolate Labradors that read:

LAB PUPS AKC CHOC 8 WKS OLD
MALES $350 FEMALES $400
ALSO THREE 9 MO OLD PUPS
STEVE- 952-XXX-XXXX.

I thought to myself, "Do I really want to get involved with Labs again? After all the bragging I've been doing on Pointers, I might have to eat my words." But I decided to make the call anyway. During the conversation, I told Steve that I was only interested in the nine-month olds. He seemed surprised, but invited me to come by and look at them on Saturday morning.

SATURDAY MORNING: IT'S PUP SHOPPING TIME DECEMBER 1, 2006

Well, I'm off and, on the way out the door, I promise Joan that I will make an intelligent decision and not buy the first pup I see. I try to contain my excitement on the forty-five minute trip out to Belle Plaine, Minnesota, and arrive hoping to meet my future hunting buddy.

THE PRESENTATION

Steve was waiting for me in the driveway and said, "I hope you came here to buy a pup."

"I came here to look and if I see something I like, I will

be a buyer." I replied.

"Which ones are you interested in? The young pups or the nine month old?"

"Actually, I'm more interested in the nine month olds. I don't have time for a pup to grow up."

Steve walked me to the kennel and said, "The two females are here, and the male is in the back pen."

Steve was your typical forties male who lived in a rural area, trying to live like a country gentlemen. He was about five feet ten, had a potbelly, and knew nothing from nothing about training dogs, but he did have nice dogs. Steve let the two Chocolate females out with an older yellow female and they started to run in circles around the yard.

"Is the yellow female for sale?" I asked.

"No." Steve replied.

I said, "Why are we watching her lead the two Chocolates on a wild goose chase?"

I could see that Steve was embarrassed and didn't have a clue what I was looking for. Finally, Steve caught all the pups and I got a chance too see them up close. I said, "Do you have a training dummy?"

"No" was the answer I expected and received. Fortunately, I had one in my van, so I went and got it. I threw a dummy for each female, but didn't like either one.

"What about that male you talked about, Steve?"

"Just wait a second, I'll go and get him."

Steve came back with the best looking Chocolate male

pup I had seen in a long time. I threw a dummy for him and he retrieved it, came running back, and jumped into my arms. I said, "This is the guy for me. How much is he any way?"

Steve said, "If he leaves in the next five minutes, he's $75."

I said, "I'll raise you to $80, since I have four twenties in my pocket."

I was shocked - the normal price for pups is $400 to $600 and a started nine-month old is typically about $750 to $1000. But who was I to argue? I was just an aged dog trainer looking for a new companion. I put the pup in the crate and Steve said, "You just made my day. Give me a deposit slip with your address on it, and I'll send you the registration papers. Yes you made my day, you made my day."

On the way home I thought, "What will I name this guy?" I thought of all the great Labs I'd owned: CIMAROC C.C. RIDER, RIDERS ANDY, GLENWATER GLORY BE, LADDS PRIDE & JOY HEIDI, GOLDEN ROD THE IV. And then it hit me, I would name him after my old hunting buddy, Paul William Lawrence, who passed away a couple of years ago. I'd call the pup P.W. and his registered name would be P.W. That was it. I'd extend my adventures with PW through this new pup. All the way home I kept remembering all the fun times PW and I had traveling the country, chasing ducks and pheasants. I kept thinking that every time I'd call P.W.'s name, I'd think of the original PW, and recall the last time we were traveling through the area.

I'M GLAD I BOUGHT A YAPPER ZAPPER

Just a couple of days before I went to look at pups, I'd ordered a bark collar. This device has a microphone hooked to a collar and then to a battery-activated zapper. Every time the dog barks, he gets a light electrical shock, so that his first bark is it. Well, this device was tailor made for P.W. because he was a barking fool. He reminded me of those big mouths in the bars who talk just to hear themselves talk. With this device, by the time Joanie got back from her trip, P.W. was a regular citizen. Now, if he ever goes non-stop barking, I just put the collar on him for a couple of hours, and he's a regular good citizen again.

BASIC TRAINING

Any dog, whether it's a hunting dog or a basic pet, will benefit greatly from Basic Obedience Training. I started P.W. out with simple retrieves and moved right there to single retrieves. From the start, he would break and go after the training dummy before I sent him, so I hooked him up to a twenty-foot rope and made him stay until I sent him. Then, when he came back and tried to go around me, I would pick up the rope and lead him in. At this point in his young life, I want him to sail out and sail in, not caring if he is steady to shoot. I've read articles from British trainers that say the best way to steady a retriever is the "No Bird Retrieve". That is, if the dog breaks, the helper picks up the bird before the dog gets there so that the dog learns that, if he breaks, he doesn't get the bird. Right now though, I don't have a helper, so I will have to work slowly into it until I do.

HAVE YOU EVER HEARD OF THE DOG WHISPERER

Jake and Linda gave me CD's for Christmas from last year's Dog Whisperer series and I can't thank them enough. The Dog Whisperer is a fellow named Cesar from Los Angeles who addresses all kinds of behavior problems with people and their dogs. I have known most of my life how to solve dog-training issues, but had no idea why they worked. I watch these CDs all the time and then put the knowledge to work on P.W. and, I must say, P.W. is coming right along. I must also remember that he is just a pup, but I fully expect him to be a fine working retriever some day. Some days, the process tires me out, but then I remember that most of the work I did with retrievers was thirty years ago, when I was in my thirties. Now, the process is a bit slower and it's not the fault of the young dog I have under my tutelage. Hopefully, accuracy will work better than speed and, in the end, we'll both learn something.

WHAT A HORSE
FEBRUARY 2007

It's February 2, 2007 and my little puppy, P.W., weighs seventy-two pounds at the ripe old age of eleven months. He sure doesn't look much like a puppy anymore, even if he still acts like one. He eats like he's a starving wild dog and, at night, it takes all my power to get him in his dog crate to avoid the cold. But, I'm really learning to live in the present moment, and my heart smiles every time I work with him. Yes, it was very sad when Heidi passed on, but she lived a beautiful life to the fullest was treated like royalty.

Yes, it's true, I'm out of the dark and into the light…and life is beautiful.

THE END

Written: February 6, 2007

THE DAY I BECAME A DOG WHISPERER

DATELINE: PAT PALMER, HEALING MOTION, WOODBURY, MN

On Thursday August 20, 2009, I was receiving my usual quarterly massage from Pat Palmer and we were discussing what I have been doing since I retired in January. I had to admit that, except for focusing on the stock market, my life has been kind of adrift. Pat said, "Weren't you going to start a dog walking business?"

I replied that I had such a hard time walking myself that, if I showed up to walk someone's dog, they would probably call an ambulance. Pat laughed and said, "Now that's a stretch. I don't think you're in that bad of shape."

We went on with the massage, talking about every subject under the sun. Finally, after an hour or so, Pat came back to the dog subject and told me what she had in mind. (Keep in mind that her massages last a minimum of three hours, so it gives us plenty of time to talk.)

I KNOW YOU CAN HELP HER OUT

Pat explained that she had a young client who was having a lot of issues with a puppy. It seemed that Andrea, who was from a large Italian family, was getting a lot of unwanted advice from people who had little or no experience with dogs. Andrea had two children, Libby, who was nine, and Theresa, who was six, and this was their first dog experience. The dog advice Andrea received from her family and friends varied from selling the dog to putting it to sleep. The latest incident was when Andrea's sister's boyfriend came calling and the dog met him at the fence with flashing teeth.

My first question was, "What breed is this aggressive dog anyway?" I thought it might be a Rottweiler, or a Doberman or a Pit Bull. But, no, the answer to that question came as quite a surprise. This trouble-maker who had friends and family at odds was none other than a nine month old Labradoodle named Lucy. Now, I have my prejudices and have never been a fan of mixed breed dogs, but I am much older and wiser now and know that dogs, like people, have individual traits. So I decided to make no prejudgments and based my evaluation on how "Lucy" presented herself to me.

I BOUGHT A NEW PHONE

In my attempt to catch up to the modern world, I bought a fancy-smancy new cell phone. I mean this phone has the internet, email, and everything else except an experienced operator. I called Andrea and left a message on her cell and she returned the call promptly. Unfortunately, I didn't know how to answer the call and it took Andrea three attempts to finally reach me. Fortunately, she was a good sport and we set up an appointment for 5:30 on Friday night. Andrea offered to give me directions but I told her that I would Mapquest the three-mile journey. Andrea agreed and I promised to be at her residence at 5:30 sharp.

MAPQUEST: HELP OR HINDRANCE

I have used Mapquest at least one hundred times and sometimes it tells you to turn left when you need to turn right. Well, it was not my lucky day and Mapquest was wrong.

YOU NEVER HAVE A SECOND CHANCE TO MAKE A GOOD FIRST IMPRESSION

Sugar beets, sugar beets, sugar beets is all that I can say; the Mapquest map made no sense at all and I had to call Andrea before I was late. I made the call very apologetically and Andrea gave me clear directions so I arrived at her home in about five minutes. I pulled into the driveway next to the garage, but parked on the street. I believe that parking in the street is a courtesy that you should extend at every place where you are a guest. The rudest thing in life is to come home after a hard day's work to find someone parked in your driveway. Andrea waved from behind the fence and I could see the two little girls and Lucy, the Labradoodle.

A QUICK AND THOROUGH ASSESSMENT

As I walked up the driveway, I saw Lucy looking hard at me and wondering just what was I doing there. I kept a very calm demeanor, went up to her, and made friends with her right away. This practice is not the practice of the TV dog whisperer because they are always saying, "you must dominate the situation." My approach is to treat the dog better than they have ever been treated before, thus presenting a very positive approach. No gimmicks and no treats because these animals were born to serve and we shouldn't have to bribe them to do their job. Andrea met me at the gate with Lucy and her two children and I suggested we sit at the kitchen table so I could share my portfolio with them. Everybody seemed eager and, best of all, Lucy the Labradoodle did not seem at all spooked. Yes, this looked like it would be a good start; and that was good news for the dog and the family.

FIFTY YEARS EXPERIENCE, HOW DO YOU COVER IT ALL?

Well, at sixty-four years old, I had been training dogs since I was eleven. Now that time frame covers a lot of dogs, so I narrowed the list down to a portfolio of my favorite dogs. The portfolio included an 8 ½ by 11 picture and a little story about each dog. I had a total of eighteen dogs featured, and the entire presentation took about twenty minutes. What the portfolio best demonstrates is that I have had experience with many different breeds, from German Shepherds to Labradors, over a long period of time. Andrea and the kids appeared interested and, when I finished, Lucy was sitting by my side.

"That's it then." I said, "If you have a leash and collar, I'll see how she responds to leash work."

Lucy responded like a champ and I quickly heeled her around the yard with her sitting every time I stopped. I promptly said, "I have seen all I need to see. I'm ready to give my final analysis."

THE FINAL ANALYSIS

"Well Andrea, there is absolutely nothing wrong with this dog and she seems very trainable. If Lucy is aggressive at times, it's because she needs daily obedience work and in six weeks you won't think it's the same dog. Here is my action plan for the next couple of weeks:

Fifteen to twenty minutes of obedience work each day for the next six weeks.

I will do an in person visit on the first and fourth week. If you encounter any problems during that time, I will come right over."

DECISIONS REAFFIRMED

Up to that point, Andrea had been told by friends and family that she'd made a mistake buying Lucy. So, to offset that, she had taken an obedience course at Petco, where they ply the dogs with treats making beggars out of them. Andrea was so happy to hear me say, "Nothing is wrong with Lucy she seems very trainable."

WHAT DO I OWE YOU?

Andrea said, "I'm all for your plan. What do I owe you?"

I've heard that sentence since I was little kid and, if I have one flaw, it's that I don't like discussing money. But I had thought this out ahead of time and I proposed that Andrea buy my book, "Colby Stories", and make her family read it. Andrea laughed and said, "I will do that. And, in addition, buy you some time with Pat Palmer."

That all was fine with me and we parted, both very content with the experience. Andrea solved a nagging problem and I proved I still have something left to give.

THE END

Written: August 20, 2009

P.W.'S FIRST HUNT

APPLE RIVER HUNT CLUB, OSCEOLA, WISCONSIN
SEPTEMBER 30, 2007

P.W. doesn't look much like a pup anymore. He's matured into quite a handsome Labrador and now weighs in at a hardy eighty-four pounds. P.W. came into my life on December 2, 2006, just four days after my beloved German Wirehair, Heidi, who had given thirteen and a half years of service, died. When I bought P.W. he was a gangly, rowdy nine-month old pup that barked incessantly. The first couple of weeks I was afraid I'd made a really emotional purchase and overreacted to Heidi's death. I kept reminding myself that it had been a long time since I'd raised any pups, but I'd owned over one hundred Labradors and, above everything else, P.W. had a sweet disposition and seemed very trainable.

THE DOGHOUSE ISSUE

When I purchased Heidi in 1999, I was talked into buying an igloo style doghouse because it would last "forever"; "forever" because the igloo was made of plastic, so it wouldn't rot or rust. However, being a child of the 1950s,

215

my opinion was that anything made of plastic equated to cheap junk. The Igloo Dog House came with a swinging door, but Heidi would never go through it. So I trashed the door and bolted carpet samples to the front of the doghouse door opening. When the cold Minnesota winds blew, I filled the doghouse with hay and Heidi stayed snug and warm inside. This system worked for the seven years that Heidi lived here, but then along came P.W. and he hated any type of covering over the front of his house. He demonstrated his displeasure by ripping the carpet samples to shreds in about ten minutes. Then he would go back into his house and dig into the hay as far as he could. These antics were sending me to the carpet store about every other day and my welcome with the carpet lady was wearing thin. It finally dawned on me one morning that P.W. is telling me to get off my billfold and buy a legitimate doghouse. So I jumped on the Internet and looked up 'doghouse plans'. There must have been thousands of different plans and configurations for doghouses. Finally, after looking for a couple of days, I came across a plan that was similar to a doghouse I had designed in high school. Yes, this would be great! In this doghouse configuration, the house was split by an entrance wall that was three quarters the depth of the house, so the dog could go behind the wall to be cozy and warm. The best part was, these plans were free! I quickly printed it out and then only I had to find someone to build it.

IF YOU NEED HELP JUST ASK SUE AT PETERSON'S COFFEE SHOP

I've always shared my ideas with my old friend, Bob Peterson, who owns Peterson's Bacon & Egg Café. Well, I had it in mind to build the fancy doghouse that I had downloaded the plans for. Unfortunately, I come from a long line of bad carpenters. In fact, I can't remember any Blanchard that was a good carpenter. Bob Peterson was well aware of this having known me over forty years, so he suggested I ask Sue, the waitress, about a doghouse builder. Sue's husband was an appliance repairman with Sears for over thirty years and, as everybody knows, all the trades people know each other. So I showed Sue the plans and asked her if she knew a carpenter who could help me. She immediately replied, "Ranger Hill. He's the man for the job."

EVERYBODY NEEDS A RANGER IN THEIR LIFE

Sue gave me Ranger's number and warned me that his wife screened all the calls. I called and Mrs. Hill did seem very inquisitive, but I ended the call by saying that I'd mail the plans and let Ranger review them to see if it was something he'd want to do. Ranger called me back in a couple of days with an estimate of time and materials and said he'd be happy to do it. We agreed on a price and I sent him a check for the materials and agreed to pay the balance when he delivered the doghouse two weeks later. Ranger called me along the way because he wanted to be sure that the shingles would match my house. I delivered the shingles and, about a week later, Ranger called, ready to deliver the final product. Ranger warned me it was heavy. It was. It took the two of us wheeling it on a wheelbarrow to get it into place. But what a magnificent doghouse it turned out to be! For starters the walls were insulated with two inches of Styrofoam on the sides, top and bottom. Also, the roof lifted off so I could clean the inside or add straw during the cold winter months. In fact, the doghouse was so cool looking that my neighbor, Fred, came over to admire it. The house was painted medium gray inside and out, but the proof of the pudding was that P.W. loved it too. No more trips to the carpet store begging for remnants - all because Sue introduced me to Ranger. Everybody who stops by and remembers the old doghouse can't believe how nice the new doghouse is.

YOU'RE A LABRADOR, YOU SHOULD KNOW HOW TO SWIM

Along about May, when it started to warm up, I decided to introduce P.W. to water over at Lake Josephine. To my utter surprise, he wanted nothing to do it. I optimistically pitched a retrieving dummy out about thirty feet, but he just stood there refusing to go in. In my fifty years of working with dogs, this was the first Labrador that didn't like water.

218

Well I had to think this one over. I didn't want to just toss him in and scare him completely, so I donned my fishing waders, took along a sixteen foot lead and walked out until P.W. was just on the edge of the water. Then I coaxed him in and led him to a spot where he would have to swim. Reluctantly, he splashed around and swam like a puppy. I repeated this process for about a week without a lot of progress. Word got around and one of my wife's friends, Lynne, said, "I hear your pup can't swim."

My reply was, "No. He just doesn't know that he can swim."

But that curt remark inspired me to think of a way to encourage P.W. to swim. Then it came to me. In a movie I remembered, every time the character was fearful he'd say, "Baby steps. Baby steps."

That's it! The next morning I took P.W. to the lake and said, "You're a Labrador and word is out you can't swim. Today that is going to change. And I am going to help you make that change."

I took the training dummy and tossed it just far enough into the water so that P.W. wouldn't have to swim to get it. The next time I threw it a little farther, then a bit farther still, until, finally, far enough to where he'd have to swim five or six feet. By the end of the summer I had a torpedo on my hands. Not only was P.W. swimming, he was making eighty yard retrieves and swimming like a seal. When I gave the command to fetch, he leapt into water with his front feet stretched out in front of him in perfect form. Now, any time I pass his kennel and say, "Let's go to the lake," he starts turning circles and getting all excited. "And somebody said you couldn't swim."

THE AKC REGISTRATION ISSUE

Right after I purchased P.W. for the princely sum of eighty dollars, the breeder said, "Just give me your address and I'll send you the AKC papers."

The AKC (American Kennel Club) papers weren't too important to me at the time, but I wanted to be able to obtain a pedigree so I could see P.W.'s ancestry. Well a couple of weeks went by and no papers, so I sent a letter with a pre-addressed, stamped envelope, but still got no reply. Then I started to call every week, but all I got was the answering machine. This went on for about ten months. Then one day I was down at the lake and a lady walked by with a German Shepherd/Lab mix. The woman said her dog's registered name was "Mississippi Mauler". That did it! My beautiful P.W. didn't have papers and this mutt did. I called the breeder at four p.m. and reached his daughter, who happened to be the co-breeder of the litter. I told her my tale of woe and she sent me the AKC registration papers four days later. When I brought in the stack of mail, I immediately recognized the return address and pounced on the letter. I opened it up and, inside, were my AKC registration papers. Very soon P.W. would be registered.

AKC PAPERS IN HAND, WHAT DO WE NAME HIM?

About five years before, my good friend, P.W. Lawrence, had passed away. P.W. had said, "Chuck-O-Luck, if you ever get a good hunting dog, name him after me."

Well that had been done, but now I had to register P.W. I wanted to think of a name that would describe them both. Then I came up with it. I'd name him "Poor Old Poverty Paul". The name came from a time when the original P.W. would be short of money and call me for a loan at the end of the month. The first thing he would say was, "Chuck-O-Luck, this is Poor Old Poverty Paul and I need a loan."

So I completed the AKC papers and a couple weeks later it was official; P.W. was registered as "Poor Old Poverty Paul".

RETRIEVER TRAINING

I have about thirty plus years of retriever training experience. I probably learned the most while working part time with a professional, Cy Sifers. But being one who always likes to learn new things, I checked out a couple new training methods. One of the new books I purchased was 'Smartwork for Retrievers' by Evan Graham, who was a very successful trainer and a student of the famous Rex Carr. I wouldn't recommend this book for an amateur, but only for the serious field trialer or professional. I used a few of the tips, but I felt the general outcome was to brainwash the dog and make it a mechanical retriever.

I was lucky enough to receive 'The Dog Whisperer' CD as a Christmas present from Linda Carter. I watched the CDs religiously and, although I felt I had pretty much known everything that the star, Cesar, demonstrated, I began to understand why the training methods worked. One key thing I learned was the correct placement of a choke collar on a dog's neck. My old method was to put the collar around the middle of the neck because that's where the dog is strongest. Cesar's method was to place the collar high on the neck, where the dog is weakest. This method has proved to be very effective. To be fair, Cesar works mostly with shelter dogs and I've worked with some of the best bloodlines in the country. Caesar does a wonderful thing working with rescue dogs and helping their owners understand how to take care of them.

By far, the most tried and true, best training book ever written is, "Training Your Retriever" by James Lamb Free. It was written in the 1950s and the methods are as good today as they were then. The book is out of print, but I got online and purchased ten copies for $1.99 each. Yes, a great book, in hard cover, for $1.99. I'll give them out as presents to friends and family because I'm sure everybody will get good use of this book.

THE PROOF IS IN THE PUDDING

Well, summer was over. It was the last weekend of

September when I decided to give Katy a call at Apple River Hunt Club in Osceola, Wisconsin. I'd been going to the hunt club alone and with friends for the previous six years. Katy and Mike ran a very nice operation and had always been very accommodating. In fact, I believe it's the only game farm that serves freshly baked cookies to its guests after the hunt. I have to admit I was little concerned about how P.W. would react to shotguns being fired and his first encounter with live birds. On the drive up I mentally went over every aspect of the hunt, hoping I was able to cover everything for what his first hunt should be.

We arrived about eight-thirty a.m. on Sunday, the 30th of September. Mike was waiting for me in the clubroom with a fresh pot of coffee. He said that Katy was in the south field planting pheasants and would be in shortly. About ten minutes later, Katy appeared looking young and as beautiful as ever. She seemed very happy to see me and said she'd planted two hens and two roosters in the south end, spaced about a hundred yards apart, about forty yards west of the pasture road. Both Katy and Mike wished me luck with P.W. and I was on my way.

I loaded up and let P.W. out of the crate. Now it would truly be proving time. We walked down the trail slowly and I was astonished at how calm he was. I fully expected him to race around like some wild man and be hard to control. But instead, he was a smooth, methodical dog that hunted close and always kept on eye on me. We came out of a small cornfield and he flushed a hen. I pulled up, the bird dropped and P.W. sat steady. I said, "Fetch him up", and P.W. calmly ran over, picked up the bird and delivered it to me. We hunted the area back and forth and P.W. flushed another hen, but this time I missed completely, so shame on me. P.W. sat there calmly looking at me and I think if he could have spoken, he would have said, "What happened? I thought you were the expert."

I headed in for a coffee break and to share the news with Mike and Katy. Both were very pleased at how composed P.W. was and were glad for my success. We went out again, made another swing and P.W. flushed another hen. Sure enough, old 'Sure Shot Blanchard' missed again. I apologized to P.W. and, since we were both tired, I decided it was time to head home.

I had more cookies and coffee and gave P.W. a bunch of water so he could quench his thirst. I cleaned my one bird, tagged it and we headed back home. I was very proud of P.W's performance and reflected back on a very successful day. I've heard of guys who paid anywhere from six hundred to three thousand dollars for a puppy and here was my eighty dollar special doing what they do - flushing birds and retrieving them. One thing I did notice was that P.W. got tired and was confused by the tall cover. I decided that, when I got back home, it was time to implement a conditioning program that included retrieves in high cover.

ALL COACHES NEED TO UNDERSTAND THEIR PLAYERS

I don't consider myself a dog trainer as much as I consider myself a coach of a one-man team. I've trained more than a hundred Labradors and each and every one of them was different. The Labrador is one of the most trainable breeds there is, but they must have confidence in you to work at their highest level. This confidence builds on successful training sessions where the dog learns and is appreciated for its progress.

A SECRET TRAINING AREA

I found a spot, not far from our home, that had tall grass cover and, within a week, I had three sessions with P.W. His progress was unbelievable! Instead of being confused by the cover, he mapped out a path in his mind and used his great nose to locate the bird. I've also been taking him to the lake because swimming is the greatest conditioner of all. Now, the dog that didn't want to go into the water in May, plunges into the water with a powerful entry and leaves a wake similar to a small outboard motor.

I truly miss my old Pointer Heidi, but this dog has stolen my heart.

THE END

Written: October 6, 2007

P.S. FALL 2010

It's becoming very apparent to me that, because of Parkinson's, I can no longer care for P.W. I put an ad in the paper, but the initial buyer is so overwhelmed by him that he offered me a hundred dollars to take him back. Then it came to me: my grade school classmate, Timothy Schmitt, has nine children and twenty-seven grandchildren. I called Timothy to ask if somewhere in that operation is there was room for a dog. Timothy delivered. He said he had a granddaughter in Milwaukee that lost her dog a year ago and might be interested.

AN ANGEL ENTERS MY LIFE

A week later, Timothy's son called about P.W. and it was a done deal. P.W. is going in two weeks. Just before it was time for P.W. to leave for his new home, I received a beautiful handwritten letter from Taylor Rae Schmitt— Timothy's ten-year old granddaughter and P.W.'s new master. P.W. arrived at Taylor's a few days later and she is delighted with him! In the weeks that followed, Taylor sent me delightful emails and pictures about her and P.W. I couldn't be happier with the way things turned out.

226

BILLY'S COFFEE CAFÉ

DATELINE ROSEVILLE, MN
OCTOBER 2009

If ever the term "bedroom community" applied, it very much applied to Roseville, Minnesota. I mean, Roseville is sleepy and aging. We have a couple of commercial coffee houses and their motto is, "Get them their coffee and get them down the road". Yes, no idle conversation, no visiting; just get the money for an overpriced beverage. A couple of independent coffee houses exist, but the proprietors have the personality of a dead board.

ALONG COMES WILD BILL

Roseville never saw the likes of Billy Bisson before. He came to town and took over the old Coffee Shop by the License Center. Word on the street was that Billy, personally, greeted everyone who came through his door. And you were a stranger there only once. Rumor also had it that Billy had had a Punk Rock Band for twenty years and traveled Canada and Europe. It seemed that things were livening up in old Roseville; I better get down there and meet Billy.

I MEET BILLY - WHAT A GUY

I walk into Billy's and spot two guys working behind the counter. I have no problem determining who Billy is. Yes, the very charismatic, young-looking man looks up and says, "Whatever you need, we got it."

I order an ice tea, Billy visits with me and, within five minutes, finds out where I grew up. As time went on, I stopped in to see Billy every day and, sometimes, three times a day. Part of this was because I am retired and part is because I'm struggling with Parkinson's. Billy was very encouraging saying his brain blew up and it took him three years to recover. In Billy's mind, you had what God gave you - nothing was a burden, just an opportunity to show the world how to overcome adversity. Yes, Billy knew everybody that came in his door and encouraged everyone to live life to the fullest.

BOOK READINGS

One day, I told Billy I wrote a book and gave him a copy of Colby Stories: Tales Of A Paperboy. Billy didn't have time to read it because he worked 100 hours a week, so, instead suggested that I do readings at the coffee shop - then he wouldn't have to read it at all. So Billy set me up with a sound system and said, "You'll sound better than Madonna."

In addition to that, he lined up a singer, Lori K., who was

only sixteen and sang like an angel. The only flop we ever had was a guy named Bill who sang while he played the accordion. He was awful - his voice sounded like a cat that had its tail stuck in the door. Billy told Bill that we were running late so he couldn't do his second set. Yes, Billy could never be hard on any talent and he bought the kid dinner. Billy was always pleased when I would do a reading because that meant thirty to forty extra plates in his till. But I think I had the most fun because, when Billy got the sound system wired and taught me how to use the mike, all my people were thoroughly entertained. To read my own material and hear the laughter was truly a joy. Thank you Billy, you're a great teacher.

I owe the success of my book readings to the support of my friends and former employers. Even my former bosses from Beltman, John and Steve, stopped by and I hadn't worked at Beltman in over three years. The last reading I did, the day before Billy closed for good, was the best. We had a guitar player by the name of Rainier, who was just twenty years old. He wrote and performed all his own music and played a 24-string, classic Gibson guitar. His lyrics were a little abstract, but his guitar playing was as good as I ever heard. Well, he also had a following of twenty to twenty-five year olds, so we had an audience that ranged from twenty one to seventy-two that night. And when a twenty-one year old woman came up to me to compliment me on my storytelling, it made my whole night. I learned a lot from Billy and will be forever grateful for the opportunity he gave me.

THE FOOD: THE BEST RUEBEN IN THE WORLD

Nobody, but nobody, makes a better Rueben sandwich in the world than Billy Bisson. I base that bold statement on my own experience and other customers who tasted one for the first time. I distinctly remember one gentleman, ninety-one years old, said that he had traveled the country, but Billy's Rueben was, by far, the best he'd ever had. Now, I have been on a stringent diet because of Parkinson's and prostate cancer, but I managed to slip away for a day and try one of Billy's Rueben Sandwiches and it truly was great.

THE VEGETRIAN SANDWICH

The Vegetarian sandwich was another very popular sandwich at Billy's. It consisted of grilled green peppers, jalapeno peppers, broccoli, onion, cream cheese, and additional cheeses of your choice, all served on whole wheat or rye. It was mighty tasty and remained a crowd pleaser the entire time Billy's was there.

THE SUPPLY RUNS

Billy ran on a very close margin and would often run out of things. The problem was that he basically ran the business alone and couldn't really get away to get anything. I sensed he was in a tough spot one day and volunteered to make a supply run. Well, that turned into one or two times a week and continued until he sold the business. I can't tell you how good it made me feel to be useful, more importantly, to be useful to Billy.

THE STAFF
BILLY

Billy was the manager, president, and CEO, plus the cook and bottle washer, and he was also the entertainment. Billy had had a Punk Rock Band in the 1970s and still had contacts. Most of the groupies were fortyish, beautiful women who would pop in any old time.

Billy also used to race motorcycles and always had the Motocross on the big screen TV.

ANNA LEIGH

Anna Leigh was the youngest of the staff at age sixteen, but she was one of the prettiest and brightest young women that you'd ever meet. She looked much older and wiser than her actual years would suggest, and, of course, the guys assumed she was older. That's when you'd see Billy's protection come out. As I got to know Anna a little better, I found out she was a writer and an artist. She showed me her portfolio and I was very impressed. How lucky I was to be surrounded by all this young talent.

JOE

Joe was a mild-mannered handsome young man who seemed to be destined for a career in healing. I complained once about the side effects of a drug I was taking, so Joe researched it. He found out that a recall was happening and, after talking it over with his mother, the advice he gave to me was, "Just quit taking it". I quit taking it, and the side effects went away. Now, what are your chances of getting that tender care from a national chain coffee house?

JOSH ROGERS AKA "THE COMMUNIST"

Josh Rogers fixed me my first cup of tea and it struck me immediately that he looked like the former Russian leader, Vladimir Lenin, so I started calling him "The Communist". Billy laughed and Josh was a good sport about it.

ANNA

Anna was probably the most mysterious woman that I have ever met. At first glance, one would think that she was a runway model – she's tall, slender, and walks with the grace of a ballet dancer. So, one day, we were chatting and I was telling her all about the Army and Anna says, "I track all that. Yes, I do Chuck, because I spent four years in the Marines as a M.P. and a dog handler."

Well, I almost fell off the chair. This beautiful creature

was a former M.P. and dog handler? We had a lot of conversations after that, mostly about the service. Then, one day, Anna asked me to help her write a speech for her sister's wedding. Anna was the maid of honor and she wanted to give her sister a good send off. I really felt honored. We put the speech together in about an hour and, a week later, Anna delivered it. Needless to say, her sister and family were delighted.

CRYSTAL

Yes, business picked up when Crystal walked through the door. Why? Because that spunky, beautiful woman could do it all. Everything just seemed to run better when Crystal was around. When we first met, it wasn't love at first sight, but once we got to know each other, we became forever friends.

BILLY'S COFFEE CAFÉ...SOLD

I was probably the last to know, but Billy had been trying to sell the business for quite awhile. Well, a buyer came along and I did my last reading on July 29, 2010. With Billy and the crew gone, it was as if my family had been killed in a car accident. Long live Billy and the crew - they will be a hard act to follow.

THE END

ABOUT THE AUTHOR

Charles "Chucky" Blanchard was born and lived in Colby, Wisconsin until he was eighteen years old. In 1963, he moved to Minneapolis, Minnesota where he has worked as a mechanic, repo-man, credit manager, bartender, and dog trainer. He is a Vietnam era veteran of the U.S. Army.

Mr. Blanchard started writing when he was fifty-eight years old and *Beyond Colby* is his second book. His first book was *Colby Stories: Tales Of A Paperboy.* He lives with his wife Joan in Roseville, Minnesota.

Both books can be purchased by contacting the author at charlieblanchard@earthlink.net
www.colbykid.com